"I shouldn't be here like this," Jo Beth murmured.

"This is where you belong," Colter said, lowering her to the blanket. Her long blond hair fanned out around her face, and her blue eyes widened as she stared up at him.

He began to stroke her—her hair, her arms, her face, her back. "Isn't that better?"

"Much. You have such nice hands." She pressed her face closer to his chest and inhaled his masculine scent.

"You are so good to touch," he said softly, then caressed her hair. "Bright as a yellow bird, and just as soft." With his index finger he traced the contours of her face. "As delicate as a flower, and just as fair." His finger outlined her lips, once, twice. Then he parted them softly and rubbed the inner lining. "Sweeter than honey from the finest clover."

Jo reached up and touched his chest, breathless from his words, his touch.

"Our time is coming, Yellow Bird," Colter said.

"Why do you call me that?" Jo Beth asked.

"In Apache legend, the wolf is all-powerful, a creature of great cunning and might. No one can tame him, save one—the beautiful yellow bird. You are my Yellow Bird, Jo. . . ."

WHAT ARE *LOVESWEPT* ROMANCES?

They are stories of true romance and touching emotion. We believe those two very important ingredients are constants in our highly sensual and very believable stories in the *LOVESWEPT* line. Our goal is to give you, the reader, stories of consistently high quality that may sometimes make you laugh, sometimes make you cry, but are always fresh and creative and contain many delightful surprises within their pages.

Most romance fans read an enormous number of books. Those they truly love, they keep. Others may be traded with friends and soon forgotten. We hope that each *LOVESWEPT* romance will be a treasure—a "keeper." We will always try to publish

LOVE STORIES YOU'LL NEVER FORGET
BY AUTHORS YOU'LL ALWAYS REMEMBER

The Editors

LOVESWEPT® • 402

Peggy Webb
Until Morning Comes

BANTAM BOOKS
NEW YORK • TORONTO • LONDON • SYDNEY • AUCKLAND

UNTIL MORNING COMES

A Bantam Book / June 1990

*LOVESWEPT® and the wave device are registered
trademarks of Bantam Books, a division of
Bantam Doubleday Dell Publishing Group, Inc.
Registered in U.S. Patent
and Trademark Office and elsewhere.*

*If you would be interested in receiving protective vinyl
covers for your Loveswept books, please write to this address
for information:*

> *Loveswept
> Bantam Books
> P.O. Box 985
> Hicksville, NY 11802*

ISBN 0-553-44033-0

Published simultaneously in the United States and Canada

---

*Bantam Books are published by Bantam Books, a division
of Bantam Doubleday Dell Publishing Group, Inc. Its trademark, consisting of the words "Bantam Books" and the
portrayal of a rooster, is Registered in U.S. Patent and
Trademark Office and in other countries. Marca Registrada.
Bantam Books, 666 Fifth Avenue, New York, New York 10103.*

PRINTED IN THE UNITED STATES OF AMERICA

OPM   0 9 8 7 6 5 4 3 2 1

This book is for
Betty Kemp, Director of the Lee County Library,
who shared her knowledge of Indians;
Dr. Michael Thompson, All Animal Hospital,
who shared his knowledge of dogs;
the library staff,
who helped with Apache research;
and the Library Board of Trustees,
who gave me support, encouragement,
and help tearing computer pages.

One

"Hold it right there."

Colter Gray Wolf thought he was hearing things. Maybe he'd been in the desert too long. He shook his head to clear it and knelt closer to the stream.

"I'm talking to you, Indian."

He felt something poke into his bare back. It was unmistakably the barrel of a gun. Automatically, he lifted his hands above his head in an act of surrender. The person speaking was obviously a maniac, and he wasn't going to take any chances.

"Don't shoot. You can have whatever you want."

There was the unexpected sound of giggling behind him, then wheezing and snorting.

"I don't want anything you've got. I just want you." Colter felt his hands being dragged down and lashed behind his back. Then the gun dug into his flesh again. "Now get up real slow and turn around.

Colter stood up and faced his captor. The person holding him captive was a bantam of a man, with a full head of curly gray hair and bright blue eyes staring out from a deeply tanned and wrinkled face. And he was holding a twelve-gauge, double-barrel shotgun. The man didn't look like a hardened criminal. Perhaps he was just frightened. Colter decided to try a friendly approach.

"I don't believe we've met. I'm Dr. Colter Gray from—"

"Quiet." The gun stabbed toward his rib cage. "If you're a doctor, I'm the Queen of England." The old man giggled again.

Colter's diagnosis was swift. Senile dementia. The old man was probably harmless, but he *was* holding a gun. Speaking slowly and clearly, as if he were talking to one of his patients, Colter tried to reason with the man.

"I mean you no harm. I'm camping two miles from here, and if you'll untie these ropes, I'll leave and you'll never see me again."

"Heck, what do you think I captured you for? I've been looking all over these parts for somebody just like you."

"Why do you want someone like me?"

"The two of us are going to be a team. I'm the Lone Badger, and you'll be Toronto. We'll make a fortune with our act."

Colter stifled his chuckle, for he knew the man didn't consider his bizarre suggestion funny. And once again he marveled at the Father Creator's wisdom. Having a loved one become senile was a devastating blow for a family, but God had added the humor to compensate.

He decided to try one more tactic.

"That's a great idea. All we need now is a horse. Why don't you untie me so I can help you catch one?"

"And let you run away? Shoot, I wasn't born yesterday. Nor the day before, either." The old man poked the gun into Colter's ribs. "March."

Colter briefly considered kicking the old man's

legs out from under him and trying to get away, but that posed too many problems. The gun could go off. Even if it didn't, even if he managed to kick the gun away, too, his captor might get to it quickly enough to shoot Colter in the back. And he hadn't come all the way to Tucson to get shot.

He did as he was told.

Jo Beth was feeling great. She'd had a successful outing with her camera—photographing the giant saguaro cactus—and her dog hadn't scared up a single rattlesnake. That was one of the things she'd been worried about when she'd taken this assignment in Arizona. Rattlesnakes. That and her parents. Sara and Silas McGill were getting old. And although her brother Rick had hired full-time help for them, she felt guilty leaving them with strangers so much. So when she'd left Tupelo, she'd brought them with her.

Her mother hated the desert, but she endured it with good grace, as she endured everything. It was her father Jo Beth worried most about. His mind was getting worse and worse. Lately he'd begun to think of himself as Rooster Cogburn. He'd even begun to talk like that crusty old outlaw.

She lengthened her stride when her borrowed cabin came into view. The Santa Catalina Mountains rose up behind it, and lights glowed in the window. It looked homey and cozy. But the lights reminded her that it would soon be dark. She hadn't meant to leave her parents alone for so long.

Her golden retriever ran ahead of her, waving his tail in the air and panting with happiness. Suddenly the dog stood still, the hackles rising on his back. Jo Beth caught up to him, bent down, and put her hand on his collar.

"What's wrong, boy?"

He growled once, low in his throat, then went streaking toward the outdoor privy. When he reached the ramshackle, unused outhouse, he began to bark.

Jo Beth laughed. "I agree with you, Zar. It's an eyesore. What can I say? The owner thinks it adds a bit of local color to the place."

Zar barked at her twice, and then put his right front paw on the door of the privy and whined. There was a muffled sound from within the structure.

Prickles of fear rose on Jo Beth's arms, but she was no coward. "Hold 'em, boy," she yelled as she unhooked her camera and ran toward the woodpile for a big stick. The first one she selected was too heavy, but the next one was just right. She hefted it in the air a couple of times for practice. She wasn't a McGill for nothing. She could hold her own with a passel of wildcats. Nobody messed with a McGill.

She ran back toward the privy. Zar was still standing guard at the door, growling. Jo Beth took the bold approach. Holding the stick of wood high above her head with one hand, she jerked the door open with the other.

A bound-and-gagged man stared at her from the toilet seat. Not just a man. An Indian. An honest-to-goodness Native American complete with braids and buckskin britches and beaded moccasins and bare bronze chest. It was the chest that held her attention the longest.

"What are you doing in my outhouse?"

She saw the man's eyes crinkle with laughter. He wriggled around on the seat and made a few muffled sounds.

"Well, of course. The gag," she said, feeling foolish.

Impulsively she reached toward the gag, and then she pulled back. Zar was no longer growling, and the man certainly didn't look like a criminal, but she didn't want to be too hasty.

"Listen, my dog will attack on command, and I'm very handy with this stick. I'm going to take off your gag so that you can talk, but don't try any tricks. Okay?"

The man nodded. It was strange how he could maintain his dignity, bound and gagged in an outdoor toilet. Jo Beth supposed it must be his heritage. Maybe Indians looked dignified at all times.

She propped her stick against the wall and approached him again, reaching behind him to loosen his gag. It was close in the shed. And the Indian was a big man. Her leg made contact with his, and her chest was pressed against his shoulder. She felt something strangely like currents passing between them. How ridiculous, she told herself. Instant attraction was a myth and falling in love was an obsolete art. She knew because she'd tried. On several occasions she'd picked out the perfect man and waited for the sparks to fly. It hadn't worked.

She quickly pulled the gag loose and stepped out of touching range. Just in case of trouble, she picked up her stick again.

"Thank you. I'd begun to think I was going to have to spend the night tied up in here."

Listening to him speak was almost a mystical experience. It was a voice that could call thunder from the sky and command the stars to shine just for him.

Unconsciously, she tightened her grip on the stick. "Who are you?"

"In San Francisco, I'm Dr. Colter Gray, but here

in the home of my ancestors, I'm Colter Gray Wolf."

"You're a doctor? How in the world did you get into my outhouse?"

"Not by choice, I assure you." Laugh lines fanned out from his eyes as he smiled. "I'm afraid I've been taken captive."

Zar was sitting at the man's feet now, thumping his tail on the wooden floor of the old privy and licking at the doctor's bound hands. Jo Beth had complete faith in Zar's instincts. She tossed her stick to the ground.

"Dr. Gray—"

"Colter."

"I'm almost afraid to ask who took you captive."

"It was a feisty old man with a twelve-gauge, double-barrel shotgun."

"I should have taken that gun from him a long time ago."

"I assume you know this person."

"Silas McGill, my father." Jo Beth knelt at Colter's feet and began to work at the ropes that bound his ankles. "I'm Jo Beth McGill, and I can't tell you how sorry I am that this happened. Dad's been somewhat confused lately. I had no idea he had gotten this bad." She looked up at him. "I *do* apologize."

"Apology accepted. There's no harm done."

A streak of gold from the setting sun fell across Colter's face. He looked like a museum bronze. Jo Beth quickly turned her attention back to the ropes. The stubborn knots came loose. She pulled the rope aside and gasped.

"Your ankles!"

There were angry red marks on his ankles where the tight rope had bitten into his flesh. She tossed the rope away and began to rub his reddened ankles. Suddenly she felt him stiffen.

"It's merely a slight abrasion from the ropes," Colter said. "Nothing serious."

"Of course." She jerked her hands away, then stood up quickly. "Let me untie your hands."

She had to lean over him again in order to get to the ropes on his hands. She felt a trickle of sweat roll between her breasts. It was too hot for a September evening in the desert. She decided that they must be in for a heat wave.

She worked silently at the tightly knotted ropes, trying to ignore the fact that she was wrapped around Colter Gray Wolf as snuggly as cellophane on a caramel candy. Another trickle of sweat dampened the front of her blouse.

Colter looked at the view closest to him—the contour of her breast. It was nicely rounded . . . and soft . . . and very, very feminine. His glance swung upward. He could see a profile of her face. It was classically beautiful, with a finely sculpted nose, high cheekbones, and full, lush lips. Her eyes were startlingly blue, and her hair was exceedingly fair.

Jo Beth McGill was the antithesis of everything Indian. She would fit right into his white world in San Francisco, but she would be a misfit in his Apache village. Not that it mattered one way or the other, he thought. He was in the desert to think, not to find a woman—especially not a blond woman.

"There." A line of sweat streaked down Jo Beth's cheek as she straightened up and held the piece of rope aloft. "You're free."

He wanted to tell her that he would never be free until he discovered exactly who he was, but the impulse quickly died.

"Thank you. May I call you Jo Beth?"

"Certainly." She stepped out of the small shack to give him room to stand up.

He started to stand, and then sank back onto the toilet seat. Jo Beth reached for his arm.

"Are you all right?"

"I've been sitting here a while. It will take a bit of time to get the circulation going again. I'll be fine." He looked pointedly at the hand on his arm.

Jo Beth's cheeks flushed, and she strode toward her camera, acting as if she'd intended to go after it right that minute anyhow. She bent over to pick her equipment up, and with her back still to him, she said, "Are you staying around here somewhere?"

"Yes. My campsite is about three miles south of here. Easy walking distance"—he chuckled—"when I can walk."

She slung her camera over her shoulder and turned to face him. His legs had finally decided to cooperate. He was standing just outside the privy door. The sight almost took her breath away. Even with a toilet for a backdrop, Colter Gray Wolf looked as if he had stepped down from the canvas of a Remington. His skin, polished by the setting sun, was all the colors of the earth—rich brown and subtle red and burnished gold. His eyes were black and vivid in a face as bold as Caesar's must have been when he'd conquered Gaul.

Honest-to-goodness sparks flew from that tall, handsome hunk right across the desert evening and landed smack dab in the middle of her stomach. Her midriff felt as if it were on fire. Of course, she thought, it could be indigestion. She'd had a rather suspicious-tasting lunch of leftovers she'd packed from the refrigerator.

Which brought her to another matter. Food. She was starving.

"You'll do no walking tonight, Colter Gray Wolf. You're coming in to supper with us, and afterward I'll take you back to your camp in my Jeep."

"That's kind of you, but I can manage from here."

"I'm not being kind; I'm trying to salve my conscience. I feel partly responsible for your predicament." She glanced toward the outhouse, and laughter began to well up. She tried to stop the laughter with her hand, but it spilled out.

"It *is* rather funny, isn't it? I can hear some of the things my colleagues in San Francisco would say."

Jo Beth regained her composure. "Then it's settled. You're coming in to supper."

"How can I resist such an invitation? Jo Beth McGill, you're almost as persuasive as your father."

"I would have used the stick if you had refused."

"Somehow I don't doubt that for a minute. But perhaps I shouldn't see your father again. I don't want to upset him."

"I promise that everything will be okay. He forgets very quickly. And my mother's cooking will make up for any inconvenience." She started to chuckle again.

"Perhaps you should have captured the moment for posterity before you released me." He nodded toward her camera. "That's some fancy equipment you're carrying."

"It goes with the job. I'm a photojournalist. Free-lance."

They had reached the cabin now. Lights from the windows glowed across the unpainted wooden front porch. One naked bulb cast an eerie glow above the front door.

Jo Beth and Colter climbed the steps side by side. She was acutely aware of him, of the lean solid lines of his body, of the silent way he walked, of that smooth expanse of bare chest. Out of the corner of her eye, she could see exactly what the porch light was doing to his magnificent skin.

She thought of turning her head just a little to sneak another peek, but sneaking had never been her style. Instead, she boldly admired him.

Colter went still. With one moccasined foot poised on the front porch, he stopped and slowly turned toward her. His face gave away none of his feelings.

The air around them was charged with currents. Jo Beth continued her silent admiration, and Colter took it in stride. Or perhaps as his due, she decided. After all, such a man was probably accustomed to being fawned over.

The moment stretched out until it was fairly humming. A small trickle of perspiration inched from under her heavy hair and dampened the side of her cheek. She thought he might say something clever to break the silence, but he remained as impassive as the snowcapped Rockies, and just as cool.

Great. She felt as if she had run five miles in the desert, and Colter Gray Wolf wasn't even sweating. He was probably used to women panting over him too.

"I hope you don't take this personally," she said.

"Should I?"

"No. It's the artist in me. I always stop to admire a beautiful view."

"Thank you."

Her temperature went up fifteen degrees. Good heavens. She'd just bared her soul, and all he'd said was *thank you.* Well, she could be just as insouciant.

"You're welcome."

She led the way through the front door. Sara and Silas McGill were sitting in rocking chairs with their backs to the door, holding hands. Sara was humming her favorite song, "Amazing Grace," and Silas was telling about the time he'd hitched a railroad car going West that turned out to be a circus wagon full of lions. The last time Jo Beth had heard that story, the wagon had been full of snakes. Her heart broke a little every time she heard his stories. They were all make-believe. Silas had almost completely forgotten that he had been a highly respected university professor with a Ph.D. in anthropology and that his only adventures had been occasional digs that turned up nothing more dangerous than a few old bones.

"Mom. Dad. I've brought a guest to dinner."

Her parents turned at the same time. Colter braced himself for the moment of recognition, but the old man merely smiled at him.

"Is he taking you to the prom, Jo Beth?" Silas asked.

Sara patted his hand. "Now, Silas. Jo Beth is too old for proms. Remember?"

Colter smiled at Jo Beth. "Are you?"

"If you're asking my age, I don't mind admitting to twenty-nine, but not a year more." She unslung her camera and placed it on the top of a claw-footed oak sideboard. "This is Dr. Colter Gray. He's camping near here. I found him in the . . ."

"In the desert." Colter walked forward and bent gallantly over Sara McGill's hand. She was tall and slim, her hair still showing that it had once been blond. Jo Beth might have her father's feistiness, but she certainly had her mother's looks, Colter thought. "I hope my being here doesn't inconvenience you, Mrs. McGill."

"Not at all. We welcome company out here in the desert," Sara said.

Colter shook Silas's hand. The old man peered at him closely. "Say, haven't I seen you somewhere before?"

"I don't think so."

"Why don't you two wash up while Silas and I set the table." Sara held herself tall as she walked across the braided rug toward the dining room. In the door she turned to her husband and called, "Silas. Are you coming?"

"It's Silas this and Silas that. . . . Silas come and Silas go." He left his rocking chair, muttering all the way to the door.

Jo Beth smiled at Colter. "He didn't remember a thing. You're safe here."

His gaze raked over her. "I'm not too sure about that."

Shivers crawled up her spine, and she couldn't blame them on indigestion.

"I can guarantee it," she said.

"I've found that life has very few guarantees."

They assessed each other again, like two wary wildcats, and then they washed up and joined her parents at the dinner table. Jo Beth discovered that Colter Gray Wolf was very adept at keeping dinner-table conversation interesting and lively. She guessed he'd had lots of practice at that sort of thing out in San Francisco. She also noticed that he was patient and extraordinarily compassionate when her father ventured off into one of his fantasies.

While her parents were in the kitchen getting dessert, she leaned closer to him.

"You have quite a bedside manner, Dr. Gray."

"That's what all the women say to me."

"And a sense of humor, too, I might add."

"In my profession, it helps."

"I can understand that—dealing with hundreds of sick people. It's hard enough dealing with only one. It breaks my heart to see Dad this way." Instinctively her hand balled into a fist.

Colter covered her hand, which lay on the white

tablecloth, and gently unclenched her fingers, one by one.

"He's not in pain, Jo Beth. He's not even aware that his words and actions are inappropriate and sometimes foolish. In your perception, he is a prisoner of his failing mind, but to him, everything seems normal. That's a compensation of our Father Creator."

"Other doctors have told me that, but none so beautifully as you. Thank you."

"It's the least I can do. After all, if you hadn't come along, I'd probably have spent the rest of my natural life in that outdoor privy." Her smile was his reward, and almost his downfall. When she smiled she looked like a mischievous angel. He didn't need any blond angels in his life right now. It was already complicated enough.

"Who wants cherry pie?"

Colter would be forever grateful to Sara McGill for chosing that moment to come through the door. If she hadn't, he might have done something rash, such as run his fingers through Jo Beth's hair to see if it was as silky as it looked.

Silas was not far behind Sara. "You wouldn't believe the trouble I went to to get those cherries. Why, I had to take my twelve-gauge gun and shoot the derned tree into submission. And while I was out killing cherries, I ran upon this Indian by the creek. . . ." He stopped speaking in midsentence and looked at Colter. "Jezebel's jewels! It's Toronto! Jo Beth, hide in the closet. Sara, where's my gun?"

Silas dropped the dessert plates to the floor, and then stared down at the broken dishes as if he couldn't figure out where they'd come from.

Jo Beth turned to her mother. "Toronto?"

Sarah shrugged. "Yesterday, Rooster Cogburn; today, the Lone *Badger*."

Hearing his name, Silas started around the table toward Colter.

Jo Beth intercepted him. "Now, Dad, this man is not Toronto. He's our guest. Don't you remember? Dr. Colter Gray."

She caught his arm, but although he was seventy-six years old, Silas was still strong. He broke loose and launched himself at Colter.

"I took you prisoner. How did you escape?"

"Dad, I—"

Colter shook his head at her. He stood up and held the old man's shoulders. "You were very brave to capture me like that. Most men don't have the courage you do."

"I'm brave, all right. You didn't think of that when you got out of the outhouse to mess with my daughter, did you?" He twisted his head to look at his wife. "Sara, help me get this prisoner back in the outhouse where he belongs."

"I'm begging you for mercy, Mr. McGill." Colter spoke with the sincerity of a contrite prisoner. "You look like a just man. If you'll let me leave, I promise that I will disappear into the desert, and you'll never see me again."

"We could have made a good team, you and me, but I didn't count on you getting sweet on my daughter. She's just sixteen. I don't want some derned savage taking her captive."

"I promise. I will not take your daughter captive."

"You won't touch her?"

"No."

"Then you can go."

"Let's seal the bargain with a handshake." Colter checked Silas's pulse under the guise of shaking his hand. It was a little fast, but not alarming. And his eyes didn't look so wild now. Cautiously, he released the man and stepped back.

Jo Beth started toward him, but he shook his head and continued his walk toward the front door. He didn't even say, "Thank you for dinner," for fear of setting Silas McGill off again.

He didn't make a sound as he walked from the dining room and through the den. He moved so swiftly and quietly, they didn't even hear the squeaky screen door close behind him.

Jo Beth stared after him for five seconds before turning her attention back to her father. He was sitting calmly at the table, cutting himself a huge hunk of cherry pie, his prisoner already forgotten now that he was out of sight.

"Have some pie, Jo Beth. And whatever happened to your guest? Didn't he stay for dessert?"

"No, Dad. He had to leave early." She glanced toward her mother. "Mom?"

"Go after him, darling."

Jo Beth ran toward the door, stopping in the den long enough to jerk the Jeep keys off the top of the sideboard. By the time she reached the front porch, she was breathless. Nerves, that's what it was.

In order to regain her composure, she leaned against a rough-hewn porch post and stared into the darkness. She sensed rather than heard the movement, and suddenly Colter was standing in the path of feeble light cast by the naked bulb on the front porch.

"I promised not to take you captive, but don't tempt me."

Two

The sound of his voice caused her to lose her breath again.

"I waited for you," he said.

"How did you know I'd come?"

"I knew."

She gazed into his face and wished God hadn't put another perfect man in her path. Colter tempted her to try one more time, just once more, to see if there really was such a thing as sparks and to find out whether she could get them to fly. She sighed. Lord, she didn't have time for sparks anymore. She didn't have time for anything except her job and looking after her parents.

"I'm here," she said. "But don't get your hopes up."

"I had my heart set on a ride with you, Jo Beth."

A hundred images came to her mind, all of them erotic.

"Riding with you could be dangerous, Colter."

"You never know until you try."

He walked closer and propped one foot on the lowest of the front porch steps.

She opened her mouth to speak, but words wouldn't come out. He rescued her.

"I'm going to have to break my promise, you know."

"Which promise?"

"Not to touch you."

He came up one more step. The porch light shone squarely on his face now. He looked every inch the savage.

"Take my hand, Jo Beth."

She reached out. His hand was warm and strong as it closed around hers. Silently, she followed him down the porch steps and out into the darkness.

"Where are we going?" she asked.

"To my camp. I'll drive."

She handed him the keys. Without speaking he helped her into the Jeep and climbed behind the wheel. Zar, sensing adventure, jumped into the back. The engine roared to life, and they set out across the desert. She leaned her head back against the seat. Sensations ripped through her—the stinging of wind on her face, the jolting of her body as the wheels took the rough terrain, the gut-wrenching anticipation of setting off into the unknown with this strangely silent man.

The drive was too short. She felt the journey ending almost as soon as it had begun. Colter turned the key, and the engine's roar ceased. The quietness of the desert night descended on them.

"Can you find your way back, Jo Beth?"

"You want me to go back?"

Instead of answering, he leaned across the seat toward her. "I'm compelled to break my promise again." He lifted a strand of her hair and watched it filter through his fingers. "It's even softer than I imagined. And more fair. As shiny and clear as the teardrops of an angel."

"Speak sweet beautiful words to me, and I'll follow you anywhere." She deliberately made the words light and teasing.

He released her hair and cupped his hand against her cheek. "Your skin is like the first snows that come down from the mountains." His hand skimmed over her face and touched her eyelashes. "And your eyes. As clear as the brook that runs through my village."

"Your village?"

"My Apache home. North. In the White Mountains." He gazed across the desert as if he were seeing a vision. There was pride in his face, and fierceness, and the briefest hint of pain, as if a battle were waging deep within his soul and he didn't know which side he wanted to win.

Suddenly he released her face and sprang lightly from the Jeep. He came around to her side and pressed the keys into her hand, "You'll be safe going home. Your brave dog will see to that." He closed her fingers around the keys and held on for a moment longer. "And I'll keep my promise not to see you again."

"That's not necessary. My father will forget this fantasy as quickly as he has forgotten all the others."

"I know he will. It's not your father I'm worried about; it's me."

"Why, Colter?"

"Because you bring out archetypal longings in me. You tempt me to ride bareback across the desert and take you captive. You inspire me to paint my face and ride into the hunt, to pit myself against the largest of the elk in order to get a warm winter wrap for you. You make me long to cover you with my blanket and make you the vessel for my children." He stepped back. "Go back to your people, Jo Beth McGill."

She couldn't disobey his command, especially since it was spoken in that glorious voice of starshine and thunder. She slid across the seat and turned the key. The engine caught, and she backed expertly away from Colter's camp.

The temptation was great to look back, but she wouldn't let herself. He was right. It was best that they not see each other again.

In the back, Zar whined.

"My feelings exactly, old boy."

She'd never met a more complex man. As she drove back through the night, she decided that she was glad he'd told her of his two identities—Dr. Gray in one world and Gray Wolf in the other. He was two men living in one skin, and in the last hour she'd become acquainted with both men. He'd been the urbane, compassionate doctor back at her cabin, but in the desert, with nothing surrounding him except wide-open spaces, he'd been a poetic, passionate Apache Indian. And both of them made her a little crazy.

Colter watched until her Jeep was out of sight. Then he dropped down onto his blanket and inspected the rope damage to his ankles. There was nothing wrong with them that a little antibiotic salve wouldn't cure. His wrists were barely marked, for he'd started loosening those bonds even as he was being marched toward the McGills' outhouse.

He got his medical bag from his gear. It was one of the few things he'd brought into the desert that reminded him of his West Coast life. When he'd left that life behind at the beginning of the summer—could the summer have passed so quickly?—he'd even considered leaving the black bag. But it was too much a part of him, just as his braids were now a part of him.

He'd started letting his hair grow a year ago, right after he'd lost a patient, Marcus Running Deer. Watching the family's quiet preparations to send Marcus on his journey into the spirit world had stirred ancient memories, had created a deep need to rediscover his Apache roots.

It had taken him months to set up his practice so that he could take an extended leave of absence. Finally he'd done it. But even after months in the desert he was no closer to knowing who he was than he had been in San Francisco.

He took a small tube from the bag, and sitting on his blanket again, began to rub the salve into his ankle. A memory of other hands on his skin came to him—small hands, slim hands, lily-white hands.

Impatiently he capped the tube and tossed it back into his bag. He'd been right to send Jo Beth McGill back to her cabin. A woman like her could make a man forget his purpose.

Jo Beth didn't see Colter again for two days. She tried not to think about him, instead concentrating on getting exactly the right shots for her magazine layout and keeping a watchful eye on her parents. Silas had seemed perfectly normal the last two days, almost like his old self; so she had let the incident with the gun go unmentioned. She knew it was the coward's way out, but sometimes she had to be cowardly in order to preserve peace and her own sanity.

She checked the angle of the sun. There was time for one more shot. While she focused her camera, her dog bounded out of sight, barking. Chasing a rabbit, no doubt. She snapped her final shots of the day and called to him.

There was no answer. She called again, louder this time. When he still didn't come, she headed in the direction he had gone. He wouldn't be hard to find. There was a small stream just up ahead, almost hidden in the lee of the mountains. If she knew Zar, he'd be neck-deep in water by now, hoping she'd come along to toss him a few sticks.

There was no need to hurry. He wouldn't go far from her. She slowed her pace and ambled along, enjoying the view. The sun was putting on a magnificent display in the west and the painted sky seemed to go on forever. She'd heard the sky was bigger in Arizona, but she hadn't believed it until she had seen it.

She came upon the stream and followed its winding curve. Suddenly she stopped. Just ahead was her dog. And beside him was Colter Gray Wolf. Man and dog were unaware of her presence. Colter was standing beside the stream, fishing pole in hand, and Zar was lying at his side, his huge head resting on Colter's foot.

It was a picture too perfect to miss. Jo Beth lifted her camera. She took wide-angle shots with lots of sunset and sky, then changed lenses and took close-ups. Excitement charged through her. It was the thrill of capturing such a breathtaking picture, she told herself as she moved in closer, her camera whirring. That profile. She had to get that sculpted profile.

She framed Colter's profile in the viewfinder and snapped. Still looking through the narrow eye of her camera, she suddenly found herself looking straight into the black eyes of Colter Gray Wolf.

"I thought you must be nearby," he said.

"I was just finishing up my day's work." She closed the shutter on her camera and moved toward him. "I wouldn't be here except that my naughty dog ran away."

Colter's smile was open and friendly. "I'm glad he did, Jo Beth. Do you fish?"

"Do I what?"

"Fish." He indicated his fishing rod. "I swore when I came to Arizona that I'd do everything the Indian way, but I seem to have acquired a taste for fish since I've been in San Francisco. Somehow piñon nuts don't satisfy that craving."

"I haven't fished since I was ten. I used to go with Rick and Andrew."

"Who are Rick and Andrew?"

"My brothers. They taught me practically everything I know."

"Including how to wield a big stick?"

"That too."

They laughed together. Zar thought the laughter meant play, so he trotted off, retrieved a stick, and dropped it at Jo Beth's feet. She tossed the stick into the water, and the dog plunged into the stream after it.

"If my supper is down there, by now it's making a fast getaway."

"Perhaps I should do the same thing."

"Afraid I'll punish you?"

"Or banish me."

While they watched each other, the evening sun dropped off the edge of the earth, taking with it the vast scarf of gold and leaving behind a veil of purple. Zar came out of the water, dripping wet, and deposited the stick beside Jo Beth. She didn't even notice him.

Colter broke the silence.

"I had a hard time that evening deciding whether I was very foolish or very wise."

"Wise, I think. What was happening was certainly a fluke. I don't believe in falling in love and all that jazz."

"You're a very modern woman."

"I am. And sensible too. I have neither the time nor the energy for anything now except my job and my parents."

"How is your father?"

"Almost normal. I wish it could last."

"I wish I had a miracle for you, Jo Beth. Out here in the desert I've come to realize that there are no miracles except those in nature." Colter closed the small space between them and put his hand on her cheek. "You're wrong about falling in love, though."

"How do you know?"

"It's one of the miracles of nature." His hand caressed her cheek. "Man and woman. They come together as surely as the big horned elk comes down from the mountains to mate with his cows."

"That's not love. That's propagation of the species."

"That's a miracle."

"Your manners of persuasion are very effective, doctor, but your arguments are not."

She broke the contact, and stepping back, called to her dog. Zar trotted to her side.

"Let's go, boy." She gave Colter a small salute. "I hope you find what you're looking for, Colter."

"Perhaps I already have."

Her face flushed. "I'm talking about in the stream. Fish. . . . For your supper."

"Suddenly, my appetite has changed. I find I'm hungry for something more than fish."

"You might try steak. There's a very good restaurant in Tucson."

She hurried away so she wouldn't have to keep up the disturbing conversation. He'd set off more of those sparks that she was absolutely certain didn't exist. Roman candles were lighting up under her skin, and firecrackers the size of atom bombs were going off near her heart.

She climbed into her Jeep, and with Zar riding shotgun, she drove back to the cabin.

Jo Beth had discovered that life was filled with small blessings. The cabin was one of them. When she had taken this assignment in Arizona, the magazine, *Wonders of the West,* had offered her accommodations in Tucson. That would have meant a lengthy drive out into the desert to do her photography every day. She'd called an old college friend, Jimmy Raifko, one of those men of perfect face and form whom she had dated back in the days when she still believed in falling in love. He was happily married now, with two kids and a wife who played bridge on Tuesdays and bingo on Thursdays and who kept Jimmy's shirts white and his socks folded. To hear Jimmy tell it, the woman was a paragon. Jo Beth was happy that somebody had fallen in love, and she told him so. He'd offered his cabin out of the goodness of his heart and for old times' sake. She'd accepted.

She parked the Jeep close to the old outdoor privy. She wondered if she'd ever see another outdoor toilet facility without thinking of Colter Gray Wolf. The great irony was that such a lowly place could call to mind such a magnificent image. Who would have thought that her first day in the desert she'd find an absolutely perfect man? A magnificent full-blooded Apache.

She shivered. She should have been worried about Indians instead of rattlesnakes.

Slinging her camera over her shoulder, she went into the cabin. Sara was knitting and Silas was reading.

Sara looked up from her work. "Did you have a good day, Jo Beth?"

"Great, Mom." She leaned down and kissed both her parents on their cheeks. "Please don't wait supper on me. I want to develop this film."

She hurried into the small storage room she'd set up as a darkroom. She rewound her film, took it out of the camera, and set to work. Some of the pictures she had taken for the magazine layout were good, but it wasn't cactus that claimed her attention. She held her breath as images began to form on the dark surface of the film. At first, it was only a faded outline, but gradually the picture came into full, dazzling focus. The landscape was of such breathtaking beauty, it almost made her cry. But it paled in comparison to the man who occupied it. Colter Gray Wolf.

She lightly traced his outline with her fingertips.

"You're too beautiful, Colter Gray Wolf. How many hearts have you broken?"

Plenty, she'd guess. He was as wild and passionate and mysterious as the ever-changing land.

She hung the pictures up to dry and left the darkroom.

Colter had a hard time sleeping that night. Seeing Jo Beth at the stream had brought back all the passions he'd tried to keep at bay. He was forty years old and had lived a full life. He worked hard, played hard, and loved hard. But never had he met a woman who had climbed so directly into his heart's cradle. It was almost as if she belonged there, as if the Father Creator had fashioned her for him and for no other.

That was absurd, of course. He was an educated, sophisticated man. He knew enough about human nature to know that physical attraction wasn't always love. But he was also Indian, and a strong believer in fate.

Rather than toss and turn, which he considered a foolish waste of time and energy, he rose from his blanket and walked under the stars. It was like being with old friends, for he knew them all, knew their names and their legends and their purpose.

When sleep began to claim him, he lay on his blanket again and fell into a deep, refreshing slumber.

He arose early, made his sparse breakfast, and climbed into an old but serviceable pickup truck, then he headed toward Tucson.

Butch Langley watched his pickup truck coming up the winding driveway, past the creosote-dipped fence posts, past the herd of cattle, past the dog kennels, and into the barnyard where he was stacking hay.

He pushed his Stetson back on his head and mopped sweat from his brow. Colter descended from the truck, and Butch marveled again at how little his friend had changed from college days. He was still as fit and trim as he had always been, and hardly a line marked his face.

"Colter. What brings you out of the desert?"

"I hate to keep presuming on your friendship . . ."

"Don't be ridiculous. After you saved my wife's life. Hell, if I hadn't flown her to San Francisco, the doctors here would have let her die. Ask me for the moon, Colter. It's yours."

"I need to borrow a horse."

"Take your pick. Though I'd advise against that black stallion. He's a wild one."

"Just the challenge I need."

He and Butch worked together to hook up the horse trailer and load the prancing, pawing animal. When the horse was loaded, they leaned against the truck and drank tall glasses of lemonade, bought from the house by the smiling Madalena Langley.

"How much more vacation time do you have, Colter?" Madalena asked.

"Two more weeks, but I could fudge a little."

"I still want to have a cocktail party for you."

"If that's your sweet way of asking me when I'm coming out of the desert, I have to tell you that I don't know, Madalena."

She patted his hand. "That's all right, Colter. I know you came out here to think, not to party. If we don't do it this time, we'll do it the next time you visit."

"You're a sweetheart." Colter kissed her cheek, then turned to his friend. "Don't ever let her go, Butch."

It was midafternoon by the time he got back to his camp at the foot of the mountains. He unloaded the big stallion and walked him around, letting the horse get used to him.

The animal laid his ears back and pawed the ground. Colter began to talk in Athabascan, the language of the White Mountain Apache. The ancient tongue spoke directly to the animal's heart. He whinnied once and turned his head toward his new master. Colter patted his muzzle.

Exultation soared through him as he vaulted onto the stallion's back. The wind sang its haunting September song as Colter and the stallion raced. The sun covered him with its kind warmth.

When the stallion had gotten used to his new freedom, Colter reined him to a brisk trot. The stream where he'd last seen Jo Beth came into sight. Suddenly an Apache poem sang through his mind: *He could not forget the woman he'd first walked with. Her song was in the brook and her face was in the sky. Earth woman, fertile and waiting for man's seed.*

He had believed that all the Indian poetry and

myths had vanished from his memory in his years of living the fast-paced life of a surgeon in San Francisco. But here in the open spaces of Arizona, he discovered that his heritage had never left him; it was waiting to be rediscovered, deep within his soul.

The woman he'd first walked with. A vision of Jo Beth hovered in his mind, and he knew that he wasn't in the desert for a challenging ride; he was there to search for her.

He scouted the length of the stream, then turned north, toward her cabin. He swung his head this way and that, scanning the landscape for a glimpse of gold that would give away her presence.

He skirted the cabin at a distance, coming only close enough to see that her Jeep was gone. The tire tracks were still visible in the sand. One set looked newer, fresher. He leaned low to inspect them, then turned the horse in that direction.

He came upon her unexpectedly. She was standing among some low scrub bushes, her camera focused on a giant saguaro cactus. A peace settled in his soul.

He sat on the stallion and watched her. With her fair coloring, she looked like a part of the sun. His loins ached with need. But for the moment, he was content merely to watch.

She was totally unaware of his presence. She hummed while she worked. It was a lilting melody that made him think of children's laughter.

He eased the stallion closer, moving in as quietly as his ancestors would have done. He saw the snake before she did. It crawled out from the bush, looking for the sunshine, and it was only a few feet away from Jo Beth.

Colter spoke to the stallion in rapid Athabascan. Horse and rider literally flew across the sand. Leaning low, Colter caught Jo Beth around the waist and scooped her onto the galloping horse. Her camera banged against his naked chest and her eyes were wide with astonishment.

He settled her securely in front of him and let the stallion gallop until he'd used his initial burst of energy. Jo Beth's hips pressed into his groin, and her breasts pressed against his arm. He thought he might ride forever.

"What are you doing?" she called over the sound of flying hooves and rushing wind.

"Rescuing you."

"From what?"

"A snake."

She turned her head. Her open mouth grazed against his upper arm. He drew the stallion to a halt.

She rested briefly against Colter's chest, panting.

"Don't be afraid, Jo Beth. I have you."

"That's what I'm afraid of."

He felt the flutter of her heart. Excitement had accelerated her pulse. It was only natural, he thought. But so was the feel of her in his arms.

She twisted around so she could see his face.

"How did you know I was there?"

"I was stalking you."

"Why?"

"For this."

He lowered his mouth to hers.

Three

Jo Beth didn't even consider resisting. Colter's kiss was as inevitable as the rising of the sun. She submitted to him, expecting a brief pleasure. She'd kissed men before, lots of men. And it was obvious that he was not without experience. But what happened there in the heat of the desert was far more than two people sharing a kiss, far more than a brief pleasure. Together they became a miracle.

When the kiss ended, she pulled back and looked at him.

"There's bound to be some logical, scientific explanation for that."

"For what, Jo Beth?"

"For feeling as if I'm riding on a roller coaster and for not wanting to get off."

"Let's take another ride."

He slid off the horse, then caught her around the waist and swung her down. Her arms went automatically around his neck, and her face lifted toward his like a flower seeking the sun.

He took her lips again, tenderly at first, and

then with an intensity that was almost obsession. This time she neither submitted nor yielded: she gave.

They felt naked in each other's arms, stripped bare of everything except their need. But there was more, more than tenderness, more than obsession, more than need. There was fire and passion between them. It bloomed so fiercely and grew so quickly that they were both caught off guard.

Colter eased his hold, and Jo Beth took a step backward.

"You tempt me, Colter."

"And you, me." He reached toward his horse and began to stroke the soft muzzle, more to have something to do with his hands than anything else.

"Were you really stalking me?"

"I didn't intend to. I intended to ride free and wild over the desert, to feel the wind in my face and the sun at my back. But that changed."

"Why?"

"It's the Apache way of courtship, Jo Beth. In the first stage, the man follows his chosen woman at a distance."

"Am I your chosen woman, Colter?"

He was silent for a long time, studying her as he pondered the question. She felt like a trapped bird, poised for flight but unable and unwilling to take off. She heard the rush of her own blood in her ears. It was the only sound in the desert . . . until Colter spoke.

"That's what I have to find out."

Her modern ideas bent and almost broke under the reality of Colter Gray Wolf. Still, she didn't have time to be anybody's chosen woman.

"I think you skipped a few stages." She kept her voice light and teasing.

He chuckled. "Are you disappointed?"

"I won't know until you tell me what I missed."

"There are three stages. In the second, I bring you presents."

"I adore presents . . . Cracker Jacks and cheese grits and goo goo clusters and those tacky bumper stickers that say things like, 'Beware of San Francisco doctors bearing gifts.' "

"I don't think my ancestors knew about goo goo clusters. What is a goo goo cluster, Jo Beth?"

"It's a Southern delicacy. A sticky chocolate candy with a marshmallow-and-peanut center. You should try them sometime."

He went so still, she had the odd feeling she was looking at a bronze sculpture. Except for the eyes. Those dark, intense eyes gave him away. They made her hot. The way he was watching her made her feel as if she had climbed on that roller coaster again.

Finally he broke the silence. "I intend to try many things with you."

Jo Beth's dog bounded out of the scrubby bushes and rubbed against her leg. Colter's horse whinnied. She didn't even notice. She was studying the magnificent, inscrutable Apache face.

"Why, Colter?"

"Do you believe in fate, Jo Beth?"

"No more than I believe in falling in love. And that's not at all."

"I'll make you change your mind." He vaulted onto his horse.

Jo Beth held up her hand. "Wait."

He leaned toward her, smiling. "Yes?"

"What is the third stage, Colter?"

"I cover you with my blanket and make you mine."

Before she could recover her breath, he had wheeled the horse and galloped away. She turned to watch. Sand sprayed up behind horse and rider, and the sound of thundering hooves echoed across the desert. Colter rode low, bending close over the horse's head, almost as if he were carrying on an intimate conversation with the animal, speaking magic words that only the two of them understood.

That was probably what he was doing, Jo Beth thought. Speaking magic. The Apache doctor had a silver tongue. He had spoken magic to her, and she was ready to give love another whirl. Well, heck. Why not? He was certainly a perfect man, perfect of face and form, educated, articulate, and sophisticated, with the added attraction of being mysterious and exotic.

Almost without thinking, she aimed her camera. But it wasn't the landscape that claimed her attention. It was Colter. A few quick adjustments, and Jo Beth had captured him forever, a magnificent bronze man, riding into the sunset.

When he was out of sight, Jo Beth loaded her gear into the Jeep, called her dog, and headed back to the cabin. All the way home she planned exactly how she would find out if love really was alive and well in the modern world. She'd brought one great party dress to the desert, just in case. She'd take Colter into Tucson, find a small hideaway with a good band, and take him onto the dance floor. She loved dancing. It was so conducive to falling in love. Then there were the moonlight walks. Nowhere on earth did the moon glow as it did in Arizona.

One or two walks in the evening could do more for love and romance than a hundred how-to books. And she'd read them all. She'd done everything the books had said: She'd used perfume guaranteed to cause swooning and toothpaste guaranteed to cause kissing. Nothing had worked. Her breath didn't rasp, her heart didn't sing, and her libido didn't tap-dance, or whatever a libido was supposed to do.

Until today.

She was smiling as she pulled the Jeep into the front yard and parked. She was still smiling when she walked through the front door.

The rope sailed over her head and settled around her chest.

"Gotcha." Her father jumped from behind the door, pulling the rope tight. "Whooee, the Long Badger has not lost his touch."

Not again, she thought. "Dad, what are you doing with the rope?" She loosened it and pulled it over her shoulders.

"Practicing. Don't you know Toronto is still on the loose?"

"He's a doctor from San Francisco, and he's merely out there camping."

"That derned Indian can't fool me. He's aiming to take my daughter captive, and I'm aiming to stop him."

Jo Beth was sidetracked for a moment by the thought of being Colter's captive. "Pull yourself together, girl." She didn't realize she'd spoken aloud until her father answered her.

"That's what I say. Pull yourself together, girl. That's what I came to the desert for—to protect you. Now you just hush that foolishness about that derned Indian being a doctor and give me back my rope."

Jo Beth looked at the man who had helped her take her first step and had taught her to tie her shoes and had sat in the front row in her elementary school auditorium, cheering while she'd played a pumpkin in the Halloween pageant. Suddenly he was the child and she was the parent. She put her arms around his shoulders.

"Come on, Dad. Let's go into the kitchen and see if we can find Mom."

Silas stared at her for a moment; then his eyes became watery with unshed tears. "Jo Beth?"

"I'm here for you, Dad."

"Jo Beth, honey. What's that rope doing in here?"

"Don't worry about the rope, Dad. Let's go help Mom."

Together they went toward the kitchen. Her fantasies of walking in the moonlight and dancing under the stars vanished in the harsh glare of reality. Family responsibility was not something she took lightly. But more than that, parental love was not something she took for granted. Silas and Sara had loved her, nurtured her, and cheered for her for almost thirty years. Now it was her turn.

As she led her dad into the kitchen, she wondered if love would have happened with Colter.

After he reached his camp Colter tethered the horse and rubbed him down. Then he climbed into the borrowed truck and headed into Tucson.

The stores were still open. He went from store to store, searching for the items he wanted. When he couldn't find them on the shelves, he asked the clerks. Most of them shrugged, some of them expressed regret, and many of them laughed.

Colter was a patient man. He settled into a booth at a small steak house and pondered his problem over a huge meal. By the time he had finished his dessert, he knew what he had to do.

He'd seen the pay phones in the foyer of the restaurant. He paid for his meal and walked over to one of them.

Jim Roman answered on the third ring.

"Colter! I thought you were in the middle of the desert. What's up?"

Colter didn't get right to the point. He wanted to lay the groundwork so his best friend would survive the shock.

"How are things in San Francisco, Jim?"

"Great. The children are rowdy, just like their mother." Jim paused to laugh. "And Hannah's positively blooming. You'll be back in time to oversee the arrival of my baby, won't you?"

"I wouldn't miss it. Besides, you might faint if I'm not there to hold your hand."

"Don't tell Hannah. She thinks I'm strong and fearless."

"I won't breathe a word. How's my houseboat?"

"Same as when you left it. Dammit, how can a doctor find time to keep all that brass polished? My boat looks scruffy by comparison. Of course, I'm rarely on it now."

"I'll polish your brass when I get back, if you'll do me a favor." Colter told Jim what he wanted.

"You want *what*?"

"You heard me the first time. Your wife's from Mississippi. Surely she can get them."

"Colter, what in the devil do you need all that for?"

"A woman."

There was shocked silence at the other end of the line, and then hearty laughter.

"Well, it's about time. I was beginning to think I'd have to take out ads for you. Tell me all about her."

"Do you have six or seven hours?"

"It's your money."

Colter began to tell his best friend about Jo Beth McGill.

• • •

In spite of her resolutions to forget Colter and concentrate on her parents, Jo Beth was disappointed when she didn't see him for three days. She looked at the empty side of her double bed, then rose to dress for another day of desert photography.

She had just tucked her shirt into her jeans when she heard the shots. Shoeless, she ran toward the sounds. They came again. Another shot, a short pause, and then two more in rapid succession.

"Dad!" She burst through the front door in time to see Silas expelling spent shells from his double-barrel shotgun. "What are you doing?"

He glanced up at her and pointed. "You see that?"

For the first time since she'd stepped onto the porch, she noticed her surroundings. Bits of chocolate and gobs of marshmallow clung to the rafters. Peanuts, cut loose from their gooey anchors, rolled around the floor. Cracker Jack boxes, splintered in half, spilled their contents over the porch. A mealy substance that looked suspiciously like grits made a white trail down the front steps.

"I *see* that, Dad. What in the world are you doing?"

"It was that derned Toronto. I know it was him. I heard a racket and peeped out my window, and all I saw was the tail end of this big old black horse. Six o'clock in the morning is no time to be looking at the rump of a horse."

Jo Beth laughed. "I agree with you, but what does that have to do with you shooting all this . . ." She glanced around the porch again, and suddenly she remembered what she'd told Colter. She liked presents—goo goo clusters and grits and Cracker Jacks. "Oh my gosh. These are *gifts.*"

"They're not gifts, Jo Beth. They're bombs. That derned Indian is planning to blow us out of our beds. Revenge, that's what it is. Just because I wouldn't let him have my daughter." He looked proudly at his handiwork. "Do you think I took care of them all?"

She looked at the pitiful remains of her gifts from Colter. "I believe you did, Dad." She touched his arm. "Let's go inside and have breakfast."

Jo Beth settled her dad in the kitchen with a cup of coffee and quietly took the gun to her Jeep. After she'd calmed her mother, she set out into the desert.

This time, she took no camera. She didn't need a camera for what she planned to do.

Colter saw her coming. He was astride the black stallion, galloping with the wind, feeling free and exultant.

He raced toward the Jeep until he was alongside. "Good morning, Jo Beth."

She couldn't hear him above the roar of the engine and the pounding of horse's hooves, but she could tell by the smile on his face that he was feeling good about his morning's work. She waved one hand toward his camp, then turned her face from his and kept on driving.

The Jeep and the stallion came to a halt at the same time. Colter slid from his horse. Jo Beth hadn't meant to do anything of the kind, but she jumped out of the Jeep and ran straight to his arms. She squeezed him tightly around the waist and burrowed her head against his chest. He smelled like fresh air and warm woolen blankets and sunshine and leather.

"If I'd known my gifts would be such a hit, I'd have brought twice as many." He pulled her closer.

"That was enough."

"I'm glad you didn't say you liked diamonds and rubies and pearls. The grits and goo goo clusters were hard enough to come by . . . express all the way from Mississippi."

"Oh my." Her chest heaved, and she shuddered.

"They were kind of funny . . . Jo Beth . . . are you laughing or crying?" He tipped her face up with his finger.

"A little bit of both, I think."

He tenderly traced the path of a tear down her cheek. "Tell me. What's wrong?"

She sniffed and gave him a crooked smile. "It was funny, really. All those goo goo clusters stuck to the porch rafters, and all those peanuts and grits rolling around the floor."

"I forgot about your dog."

"It wasn't Zar. It was Dad. He saw you leave the gifts, then he went outside and blew them to pieces with his shotgun." She hiccuped twice, and the tears began to come in earnest. "I took the gun."

Without a word Colter lifted her and carried her inside his dwelling. It was a modern version of the ancient Apache wickiup—poles lashed together in a circle, covered over with large deerskins, purchased at great expense by Colter just for the purpose of re-creating a part of his heritage.

The flap of deer hide closed behind them. In the semi-gloom of the tepee, he sat on his blanket, still cradling Jo Beth in his arms.

"There are modern medicines for anxiety . . ." he said.

"I don't have anxiety."

". . . but I never prescribe medicine when a little tender loving care will do just as well." He smoothed back her hair. "Or better."

"Colter . . ."

"Lean on me, Yellow Bird." He began to stroke her—her hair, her arms, her face, her back—with firm loving strokes that were balm to her soul. "There now. There. Is that better?"

"Much. You have such nice hands." She pressed her face closer to his chest and inhaled his masculine scent.

"You are so good to touch." His hands roamed over her face once more.

"I shouldn't be here like this."

"This is where you belong." Colter lowered her to the blanket.

Her long hair fanned out around her face, and her blue eyes widened as she stared up at him.

"Is this part of the cure, doctor?"

"This is personal." Propped on one elbow, he gazed at her for a long while, then slowly lifted a strand of golden hair and let it sift through his fingers. "As bright as a yellow bird, and just as soft." With his index finger, he traced the contours of her face. "As delicate as a flower, and just as fair." His finger outlined her lips, once, twice. And then he parted them softly and rubbed the moist inner lining. "Sweeter than honey from the finest clover."

She reached up and touched his chest. He was wearing a shirt of soft deerskin, open at the neck and laced together with long leather string. She eased her hand between the lacings and rested her palm on his bare skin. It was smooth and firm and warm.

"Colter, you make everything I believe seem a lie."

"Perhaps they weren't really beliefs, only rationalizations."

"I don't know. I don't seem to know anything anymore." Her hand circled on his chest. "You feel so solid . . . so real . . . so good." Her face clouded over and she started to withdraw her hand.

"Don't." Colter covered it with his.

"I must." He released her, and she put her hand at her side. "I came here to tell you that it won't work. The presents, the courtship . . . even the kisses."

Colter listened quietly, instinctively knowing that she needed to talk.

"Just look at me." She sat up and shook out her hair. "Wallowing on your blanket like a wanton." She gave him a wry grin. "Could I get you to believe that it sometimes works, but I don't want it to?"

"I believe that, Jo, and I understand."

"You do?"

"Yes. You don't want to neglect your parents." He smoothed back her hair. "I've seen these situations—the parents getting older and sicker, needing more and more attention, and the adult children struggling with their consciences, trying to decide what is best and what is merely selfish." He put his hands on her neck and began to massage the tense muscles. "You're not selfish, Jo. I know that. But neither should you be self-sacrificing."

"I'm not a martyr, Colter. What I do for my parents is done out of love."

"I know that too." He kissed her cheek. "Lie back down, Jo, on your stomach."

She arched her eyebrows at him. "At this time of the morning and with our clothes on?"

He roared with laughter. "Don't tempt me, lady." Still chuckling, he eased her back down on the blanket. He bent close and looked directly into her eyes. "Our time is coming, Yellow Bird."

"Why do you call me that?"

"In Apache legends, the wolf is all-powerful, a

creature of great cunning and might. No one can tame him, save one—the beautiful yellow bird. You're my Yellow Bird, Jo."

She cupped his face. "Can I change my mind about this not working, Gray Wolf?"

"Yes. You can change your mind . . . tomorrow."

"Why not today?"

"Because today you're going to do just what the doctor orders. First, a massage, then a nice quiet day doing whatever makes you happy. What makes you happy?"

"Reading a good book, listening to music, walking in the woods, playing with my dog, sitting in the sunshine and refilling my inner vessel."

"I like you, Jo."

"I like you, Colter." Her fingers traced his high cheekbones. "And what will you be doing while I'm lazing around being happy?"

"I'm going to pay your father a visit."

"You can't." She tried to sit up, but he held her down.

"I'm going as a doctor, Jo. There are certain mild medications that can be used for people like Silas."

"I don't want him to be a zombie. He's always been bright and vital and active. I want him to go fiercely into the night." Even lying down she spoke with great passion and conviction.

"He will. I promise you that." Colter gently rolled Jo Beth onto her stomach.

"What?"

"Just what the doctor orders." He tugged at her waistband and eased his hands underneath her shirt.

Four

She shivered as his hands skimmed over her bare skin.

"Your trapezius muscles are very tight, Jo." His fingers were firm but gentle as they worked at her shoulders. She felt the knotted muscles begin to loosen. His hands moved down her arms. "And your deltoids."

"I like it when you talk sexy, doctor."

"And I like it when you laugh. Do you know that your laughter reminds me of children at play?"

"What a lovely thought."

He accepted her compliment silently and continued to massage her back. He knew the name of every muscle he was touching—the deltoids, the biceps, the pectoralis major. Ahh, he thought. The pectoralis major. With the heels of his palms resting flat on her back, he massaged the soft silky flesh at the sides of her breasts.

She sighed.

"Does that feel good, Jo?"

"What you do with your hands is magic."

What he was doing with his hands would be

more than magic if he didn't move them. What he was doing with his hands right now, he decided, was pure seduction.

He left her intoxicating pectoralis major and placed his hands flat just above the waistband of her jeans. With long, even strokes, he rubbed her from waist to neck, over and over, until she felt limp and relaxed under his fingers.

He withdrew his hands and smoothed her shirt down.

"Jo," he said softly.

She didn't stir. With one hand under her cheek and her hair spread like warm honey over his blanket, she was fast asleep.

He felt a glow of satisfaction. Jo Beth had paid him the ultimate compliment: She had trusted him enough to fall asleep in his tepee. He studied her. She was wonderfully fashioned—lean torso, slim waist, and long trim legs. He smiled. She was barefoot.

Once again he felt good. She had come straight to him, not even taking the time to put on her shoes.

He carefully lifted her feet, one at a time, and wiped the dust off the soles. Then he leaned down and kissed the milky white, blue-veined skin where her left foot arched.

"Rest, my Yellow Bird. Dream of me."

She stirred in her sleep, smiling. Then she pressed closer to his blanket, and her breathing became even once more.

Colter changed shirts quietly, tossing aside the buckskin and substituting an ordinary blue denim. Next he tucked his braids under an old San Francisco Giants baseball cap, picked up his medical bag, and left his tepee.

•　　•　　•

Jo Beth was awake when he returned from her cabin. She was sitting cross-legged in the sunshine beside the flap of his tepee, her jeans rolled up and her face turned toward the sun. And she was smiling.

He climbed from the truck and walked toward her.

"Hi. You look different with your braids tucked under that cap."

"More professional?" He dropped to his knees beside her.

She assessed the denim shirt, open at the throat so that his fine bronze chest showed through; the well-used, oft-washed jeans, getting threadbare at one knee; the faded baseball cap.

"For San Francisco, maybe, but not for Mississippi."

He smiled. "Tell me about Mississippi. I've been there only once."

"What city?"

"Greenville. My friend Jim Roman married a Delta woman, Hannah Donovan."

"I can't believe you know the Donovans!"

"Only Hannah. I've met the others, of course, but I don't know them."

"Hannah's brother Jacob is my brother Rick's best friend. That makes us almost friends."

"Almost friends and nearly lovers."

They exchanged a long look. Her face glowed with sunshine and laughter and anticipation. He put one palm on her sun-warmed cheek.

She covered it with her own. They stayed that way for a long while, in silent awe of the thing that was happening between them—the magic, the beauty, the miracle.

Finally, Jo Beth spoke. "You saw my father?"

"Yes. He accepted me. In fact, his mind was

relatively clear. I gave Sara a mild medication to use when he is agitated and out of control."

He took off his baseball cap and placed it on top of his medical bag. Just that single gesture, that releasing of his braids, made him look fiercely Indian.

Desire spiraled through Jo Beth, and need, a need so great she almost cried out with the force of it. Why had she come to Colter this morning? she wondered. Was it only to tell him to stay away? If there was one thing she prided herself on, it was her honesty. And it was time to be honest with herself. She had come to Colter because of who he was. Not just a doctor, not just a man. Colter Gray Wolf was a man of strength and courage and kindness and humor. He'd shown his generosity of spirit in dealing with her parents. She'd hungered for him as naturally as the earth hungered for spring rains. And she had not been disappointed. He'd covered her and refreshed her.

She reached out and touched his face. "Thank you."

"You're more than welcome."

He caught her hands and stood up, pulling her with him. "Have you ever ridden bareback, Jo Beth?"

She gave him an arch smile. "I'm not sure I should answer that, on the grounds that it might incriminate me."

He roared with laughter. "I'm speaking of horses."

"Well, I was too."

"Of course you were. I never question the word of a sweet little Yellow Bird." He patted her flushed cheek.

She stared into his eyes until she thought she might drown in all that blackness, and then she turned to study the tethered stallion.

"Surely you don't mean that beast? He's monstrous."

"He's a stallion, and really quite tame if you know how to handle him."

"My brother Andrew loves horses. He was always trying to teach me to ride, but I kept ending up in the dirt."

"Jo, I promise you won't end up in the dirt." He let his gaze sweep over her. "On second thought, I take that back. You'll end up in the dirt only if I want you to."

"I'm not sure I can trust a fast-talking wolf like you."

"You can trust me for today. After today I make no promises."

"Why can I trust you for only one day?"

"It's my gift to you."

"One Dad can't destroy with a double-barrel shotgun." Her smile was bittersweet. "I would love to accept your gift, Colter, but I can't."

"Why can't you?"

"I should get back and see about my parents. I should finish my work so I can get them out of the desert and back home."

"Jo, listen to me." He bracketed her face with his hands, sliding his fingers into her shiny hair. "You can't continue to give if you are empty. Let me refill you." He felt her skin heat up, and he smiled. "Let me refill you with laughter and happiness and a giddy sense of fun, so you will return to your work and your obligations refreshed."

She took a moment to think about all he had said, and then she smiled. "You are a man of great wisdom. I accept."

"Good." He took her hand and led her back into his tepee. "Now, no more serious talk. Just fun."

He reached into his stack of supplies and took

out a basket, bright with red and blue designs of leaping deer and festive with leather fringe.

"It's beautiful," Jo Beth said.

"An Apache burden basket. And it's going to carry quite a burden today, because I'm starved."

She helped him pack food for the picnic, then watched as he slung the basket over his shoulder and went to untether his horse. The animal was skittish around her, and Colter spoke to him in a strange fluid tongue. After he had gentled him, Colter slung a blanket across the stallion's back and turned to Jo Beth.

"It's time."

"Can't we walk? Or go in my Jeep?"

"Don't be afraid. I'll be right here. You can hold on to me." He caught the stallion's mane and vaulted onto his back. "Take my hand, Jo Beth. Trust me."

"I do . . . and I'm not afraid of anything."

She took his hand, and he swung her up behind him. She wrapped her arms around his waist.

"Hold on tight, Jo."

He spoke those strange musical words again, and the animal moved with a grace that was more sensation than motion. Colter rode close to his horse, perfectly attuned to the animal's movements, and Jo tried to move when Colter did. For a while she was stiff and uncertain, but soon she began to relax and let herself flow with his rhythm.

The hoofbeats pounded the hard desert floor and the wind sang through her hair. At first it was a desert song, a melody of dusty packed earth, distant mountains, and shy animals hidden among the rocks. Then the music changed. It became a siren song, an intoxicating melody of strong, solid muscles and rich, masculine smells—leather and sweat and denim.

She cuddled her cheek against Colter's back. His muscles tensed, but he kept on riding, riding with the wind and the thunder of hoofbeats. Jo opened her mouth and pressed her tongue against his shirt. He tasted salty . . . and wonderful.

She took another taste.

The stallion veered sharply. Colter raced the last few yards toward the foothills of the mountains and came to an earth-scattering stop beside a stream. Sand and small stones spewed up around them. Before the dust had settled, Colter had dismounted, taking Jo with him.

His face was fierce as he bent toward her. He claimed her mouth quickly, urgently. She clung to him, still feeling the rocking motion of the horse, still intoxicated by the heady siren song and the nearness of her own personal doctor.

Passion burst into full bloom, as it always did with the two of them. Colter groaned and dragged her closer, cupping her hips and fitting them into his.

"A small taste of heaven," he murmured into her mouth, "before the picnic."

She laced her fingers around his neck. "Colter . . . don't talk. . . . Kiss."

He did. There in the desert with the stallion snorting softly and nudging Colter's back, they refilled each other. He gave her strength and power and passion; she gave him softness and tenderness and desire. He gave her joy; she gave him happiness. And they gave each other another miracle.

When the kiss became so rich they had to break apart to savor it, Colter gazed into Jo Beth's face.

"Tomorrow, my Yellow Bird, we finish what we started."

"How can you be certain?" she whispered.

"My heart understands yours, and . . ."

"And?"

"My time in the desert grows short, too precious to waste."

"I'll be leaving soon too."

"How soon?"

"A few days. A week at the most."

"Then, Jo, let's finish today so that tomorrow will come quickly."

Colter tethered the horse and they unpacked the picnic lunch. Sitting on the Indian blanket that had recently been their saddle, they shared a lunch of cheese and bread and beef jerky. Afterward, they rolled up their jeans and waded in the stream.

Their laughter echoed across the wide-open spaces. The September sun spilled its warmth on them, and they were happy.

With water swirling around her knees, Jo Beth stood in the stream and looked at Colter.

"I didn't know how much I needed this . . ." she said as she spread her hands wide to encompass the stream, the Indian blanket with its gay design and its burden basket, the enormous sky, even the stallion, ". . . this frivolous frolic." Her laughter pealed like merry children at play.

"You like frivolous frolic, do you?" Colter's eyes gleamed with mischief as he bent over and scooped up a handful of water. "How about frivolous, *wet* frolic?"

With a flick of his wrist, he dashed the water toward her. It wet the front of her jeans.

"You want a water fight, do you? You're messing with a pro."

Lifting one foot then the other high out of the water, she ran behind him and splashed water over his back. He turned and aimed a handful at the front of her blouse. Laughing, she bent over and churned up a wave large enough to soak his jeans.

She stood with her hands on her hips, triumphantly surveying her handiwork.

"You should see yourself, Colter." She laughed. "You're soaked. I won."

He smiled at her, his black eyes roaming over her water-sprinkled face, her wet shirt, her damp jeans. Suddenly the smile faded, and his eyes became hooded.

"No. I think I won."

With two strides he closed the space between them. He cupped her breasts through the damp shirt, lifting and molding them with his hands.

"And earth mother opened for the father sky, offering her ripe womb for the life-giving rains."

"Colter?"

"Yes?" He caressed her, pressing the wet fabric against her soft skin.

"What is that?"

"Apache poetry."

She reached out and placed her fingertips against his lips. "It's beautiful; you're beautiful."

He was as still as only he could be, with a waiting, watchful stillness that made her breath catch high in her throat.

"Jo Beth, you are earth, I am sky. You will open, and I will fill you with my rain."

"Fate?"

"Yes." He put his hands on her shoulders and gently drew her toward him. "Come, Yellow Bird."

She moved toward him, willing at that moment to follow him to the moon, the sun, the stars, the end of the desert, to wherever he wanted to go. He draped his arm around her shoulders and led her toward the bank. When they reached the edge of the water, he lifted her and laid her on the blanket. Then he leaned down, propped on one elbow, blocking out the sun.

With one hand, he wiped the droplets of water from her face. "I'm glad you came to the desert."

"So am I." She caught the front of his shirt. "Colter. Lie down beside me."

He lay beside her, their damp legs touching, their wet shoulders pressed close together.

"The sun will dry us quickly," he said.

"It feels good."

"*You* feel good."

She rolled onto her elbow so she could look down at his face. "Why are you such a nice man?"

"For you, I'm keeping the beast tightly chained."

"For today?"

"Yes." He smiled. "Only for today."

She lay beside him again and folded her hands under her head. They were content to lie together, not talking, letting the sun warm their skin and dry their clothes.

As the afternoon waned, they began to talk. Colter told her about his houseboat in San Francisco and his childhood home in the White Mountains. In a voice full of Apache cadences, he talked of the rituals, the myths, the poetry.

"Your voice is like music, full of poetry and passion," she said.

"You bring out the music in me." His gaze wandered over her. "And the passion." He took her hand and pulled her up from the blanket. "We're almost dry; let's ride."

They repacked the burden basket, threw the blanket across the stallion's back, and rode. Astride the racing stallion and clinging to Colter's back, Jo Beth felt a marvelous freedom and a sense of well-being.

"Colter, thank you for this day. It has been a beautiful gift." She spoke loud enough to be heard over the stallion's staccato hoofbeats.

"I will give you many beautiful days as gifts."

"We'll see."

As they galloped across the desert she wondered how Colter would be able to give her many beautiful days if he was in San Francisco practicing medicine and she was in Mississippi taking care of her parents. But she didn't want to spoil her gift by pointing that out. She'd just drift along and see what happened. She smiled. It was the first time she'd felt like drifting in a long, long time. She had Colter to thank for that.

And when they reached his camp, she did. He slid off the stallion and lifted her down. She put her arms around his neck and held him close.

"You are a very special man, Colter Gray Wolf. Thank you."

"You're a special lady, Yellow Bird. It was my pleasure."

While he took care of the stallion, she folded the blanket and carried it along with the burden basket inside his teepee. Colter kept his dwelling place immaculate, clean and unmussed, even after their hasty preparations for the picnic. It was much like the man, she thought, for she had never seen him look anything except immaculate and dignified, almost as if he had been sculpted instead of born. Whether he was bound in an outdoor privy or sitting astride a stallion with the wind blowing his hair or standing in the stream with water soaking his clothes, Colter always reminded her of a perfect museum bronze. His tight control might have been scary if she hadn't known that he was a man of fire and passion and poetry.

She didn't hear him enter the tepee. Only when

she saw a patch of sunlight on the ground was she aware of his presence. She turned slowly to face him, and he lowered the deerskin flap.

"I was admiring your camp. It's like you—neat and unmussed." She crossed the small space that separated them. "Are you always like that, Colter, in complete control?"

"Until now, Jo Beth. Until I met you." He pulled her into his arms and gazed down at her. "You are rocking the foundations of my life. The things I'd hoped to find in this lonesome place don't seem to matter anymore. All that matters is you."

His hands were gentle as they bracketed her face. His lips were tender as they brushed across hers.

"Go now, quickly, before I lose all my nobility."

"You could never do that."

With his arms wrapped around her, he swayed, holding her body pressed tightly against his. "Ahhh, Yellow Bird. I'm on the edge of a cliff, about to plunge over."

She rested her head in the curve between his cheek and his shoulder. With her open mouth, she pressed kisses against his throat.

"You tempt me to stay, Colter . . . forever."

They swayed together, their heartbeats joined in perfect rhythm. Finally, Jo Beth pulled out of his embrace.

"Good-bye, Colter."

He smiled. "Only for a little while."

He held the flap open, and she left his tepee. Standing in the opening, he watched her climb into her Jeep and drive away. Then he went inside and began his preparations for the coming night.

The sun was lowering in the west by the time

Jo Beth arrived at her cabin. Silas and Sara were waiting for her on the front porch swing.

"Your Dr. Gray is a nice man, Jo Beth," Sara said.

"Humph." Silas set the swing into motion with his foot. "He's a wolf parading in sheep's clothing. He didn't fool me for a minute."

Jo Beth sat on the steps sideways so she could face her parents. "How's that, Dad?"

"Shoot, I knew it was Toronto all along. If I'd a had my gun, I'd a filled his britches with bird shot and sent him on his way. How can I take care of my family without my gun? That's what I'd like to know."

"Now, Silas." Sara patted his arm.

Months of dealing with Silas had taught Jo Beth it was best not to argue with him. She'd learned the hard way that to placate was better than to disagree.

"Dad, I appreciate what you've done for me, but I have Zar for protection." Hearing his name, the big golden retriever rose from his napping place on the front porch and came to sit beside Jo Beth.

"A fat lot of good he'd do against that sneaky Indian. Where's my gun?"

Desperation is often the father of inspiration. Relief flooded Jo Beth as her inspired idea took hold.

"I don't need you to protect me, but I really need your help, Dad."

"How's that?"

"If you could help me with my photography, I could finish this job quickly. Do you think you could learn to use one of my cameras?"

"I could learn to use a derned pipe organ if somebody would teach me."

With Sara looking on and providing encouragement, Jo Beth taught Silas about focusing and shutter speeds and exposure. After the lesson, Silas walked around taking shots of the dog's tail, the porch rafters, and his wife's feet. Jo Beth and Sara left him standing on the porch, happily clicking away at the outdoor privy.

Evening came quickly to the desert. The sun dropped over the western rim of the earth, and the sky changed from pink to red to deep purple. The long shadow of the mountain melted into the surrounding darkness, and Jo Beth sat on the front porch swing, at peace.

Out of the darkness came the cooing of a turtledove. Jo Beth stopped swinging to listen. The call sounded once more. How could that be? she wondered. A dove in this barren place with no forests nearby?

There was a small rustle, and Colter stepped out of the darkness. Jo Beth put her hand over her heart.

"You startled me."

"I didn't mean to." He propped one foot on the front porch steps and watched her.

"How did you get here? I didn't hear an engine, or a horse either."

"I ran."

He didn't look as if he had been running. In the narrow light provided by the moon, he was as unhurried and unruffled as if he had stepped from an air-conditioned limousine. Even his chest, bare in the moonlight, didn't show a sign of perspiration.

Jo Beth set her swing into gentle notion, rocking and looking at Colter. She had learned silences from him, so she waited for him to speak.

He didn't for a long while, content to watch the play of light over Jo Beth's fair hair. The creaking of rusty hinges on the swing was the only sound. Finally Colter spoke.

"While I was running, I decided that a perfect day should have a perfect ending." He climbed the steps and moved across the porch until he was standing in front of her. Catching the chains, he brought the swing to a halt. "A perfect ending demands a perfect woman."

"I'm not perfect, Colter."

"You're close enough."

He sat down beside her, resting his arm along the back of the swing. His forearm brushed the sensitive skin at the back of her neck. That small contact was enough to make her shiver.

He noticed and smiled. With one moccasined foot he set the swing into motion again.

"I'm glad you came, Colter. I haven't thanked you properly for what you did today."

He smiled. "How does a Mississippi girl properly thank a slightly confused San Francisco doctor?"

"Like this." With a wicked grin, she shook his hand.

"Let me rephrase that question. How does a pretty Yellow Bird thank a hungry Gray Wolf?"

She reached toward the back of the swing and pulled his arm down over her shoulder. Then she slid across the slatted swing and took his face between her hands.

"Like this."

Five

She kissed him with exquisite tenderness. The swing continued its rocking, and across the porch Zar thumped his tail on the wooden floor. The stars moved through the velvet blackness of the heavens, and the moon kept its course across the vast sky.

Without breaking contact, Colter shifted Jo Beth onto his lap. One foot renewed the motion of the swing so that they swayed together, gently, like two night-blooming flowers in a friendly breeze.

They finally reached a break point, and they had to stop or plunge over the edge.

"Stopping is pain," he said, his mouth only a fraction of an inch from her lips.

"My parents are inside."

"And I'm still being noble." He settled her head against his chest, stroking her hair and swinging. "I had no idea that hair could be such a powerful aphrodisiac."

"Is it?"

"It's always the first thing I notice about you . . . this bright and shining cascade of hair."

She rested her hand on his chest, right over his heart, and sat quietly, content to listen to the mystical music of his voice.

"Before I came to Arizona, I had almost given up running. For one thing, I didn't have time. But the need was there . . . Apaches have always been great athletes, you know. Swift runners."

Zar ambled over and rubbed against Colter's legs. Colter bent down to pat the dog's head, then settled back with Jo Beth in his arms.

"Don't stop, Colter. The sound of your voice is soothing."

"Your cabin is dark tonight."

"My parents went to bed early, and I wanted to sit in the dark."

"At first I thought all of you had gone to bed, and then I saw your hair, shining through the night."

She leaned back to look at him. "You're joking."

"No." He smiled at her. "So I stopped and called to you."

"I didn't hear you."

"Did you hear a turtledove?"

"That was you?"

"Yes."

"Colter, you're full of surprises."

"I'm glad you mentioned surprises." He made an expert maneuver, holding on to her while reaching into his pocket. "I have another gift for you. One slightly damaged goo goo cluster."

She stared at the shiny wrapper in his hand. It was crumpled and mashed from being in his pocket.

"I think I'm going to cry." She put her hands to her cheeks.

"You don't like mashed goo goo clusters?"

She saw the teasing light in his eyes. "I love

them, and I've decided I can't eat and cry at the same time." She took the candy and peeled back the wrapper. "What's more, I'm going to share."

She broke off a tiny bit of candy and held it to his lips. He took it all into his mouth—the chocolate, the marshmallow, the peanuts, and two delicate fingers. He wrapped his tongue around her fingers.

"Hmmm, delicious." With his mouth full, his words were garbled, but she understood them nonetheless.

"There's more where that came from."

He released her fingers and swallowed the candy. "Eight more, if I'm not mistaken."

"I'm talking about the candy."

"I'm not."

He lifted her hand and kissed the palm. Then he took her fingers into his mouth, one by one, savoring the texture and the special taste of her skin.

A flush heated her skin. Even after he let her fingers go and stood up, she still felt warm and languid.

"Tomorrow evening, Yellow Bird, I'll come for you."

"I don't know . . ."

"You will hear my signal and come to me."

"The turtledove?"

"And you will ride with me."

He disappeared as quickly as he had come, blending into the darkness so that she couldn't tell his direction. Instinctively she knew he was running, and she leaned forward to catch the sounds. But not a single footfall marred the silence of the night.

She stayed in the swing a while longer, enjoying the luxury of doing nothing, then went inside to bed.

• • •

"Dad-blamed it, Jo Beth. You're slower than Christmas." Silas moved from one cactus to another, taking pictures as fast as he could. "We've been here all morning, and I'll bet I've made twice as many as you."

"Four times." She focused carefully, never looking up.

"Is that right? Hot dern, I'm gonna get rich."

He moved around behind Jo Beth, snapped a great shot of the sky, then trained his camera on the western horizon. Colter and his stallion came into view.

"I've got that sucker now." Silas frowned into his viewfinder as Colter came closer. "Hold it right there, Toronto."

Jo Beth whirled around. "Colter. What a pleasant surprise."

He smiled at her. "I knew I'd find you out here somewhere." He held up the burden basket. "I brought lunch . . . enough for three." He dismounted. "Hello, Silas."

"Stay right where you are." Silas was clicking his camera furiously.

"Dad, what in the world are you doing?"

"Collecting evidence. I'm gonna send these pictures to my son." He glared over the top of the camera at Colter. "Rick's a private eye. He'll know just what to do about you. . . . Shoot, I'm out of film." He went to the Jeep to reload his camera.

"I'm sorry," Jo Beth told Colter.

"It's better than being tied in the privy." He caught her hand. "How are you?"

"Busy. Happy. And glad to see you."

"Ready for a lunch break?"

"Yes."

They let down the tailgate of the Jeep, and Colter unloaded the folding canvas chair Jo Beth had brought for Silas. Silas hopped around them like a bantam rooster, aiming his camera and yelling, "Gotcha."

Colter took it all in stride, and Jo Beth smiled, but every time her father yelled, her heart broke a little. He needs me, she thought. Now, more than ever.

"Dad, let me put your camera away so you can eat lunch."

"He just wants to get his hands on it so he can steal the evidence." Silas, his Panama hat flapping with every movement of his head, nodded at Colter.

"Silas, I promise not to touch the camera."

"Humph. A lot of good your promises are. You promised not to take my daughter captive, and look what's happened."

Colter thought Silas must be more astute than he seemed, for at that very moment he was thinking ahead to the night, planning for the moment when he would take Jo Beth to his camp.

"Dad, this is Dr. Gray. Remember?" Jo Beth took her father's hand and led him to the canvas chair. "He doesn't want to take anyone captive. He's our friend, and he's brought us lunch."

Colter prepared a paper plate and brought it to Silas.

"What is it?" The old man eyed the food suspiciously.

"Fresh fruit and fish I caught this morning."

Silas took a bite and smacked his lips. "Toronto, if you ever decide to give up being a savage, I can get you a job as a cook. I have this friend back home in Mississippi. Owns this little old restaurant—the Lonesome Pig, it's called. We're buddies, the two of us. One time . . ."

Colter and Jo Beth sat on the tailgate, eating their lunch while Silas talked and talked, spinning his fantasies. With Silas's voice droning in the background, they carried on a quiet conversation.

"The fish is delicious, Colter."

"I have a confession to make: I didn't cook it."

"I know you're full of surprises, but don't tell me you have a cook stashed away in that tepee."

"No. I carried some fish to your cabin this morning, and when Sara found out what I was going to do, she insisted on cooking it." He smiled. "I think she likes me."

"I'll have to warn her about San Francisco doctors bearing gifts."

"I've run out of gifts, Jo Beth." He took her hand and kissed her fingertips. "The second stage must come to an end." She caught her breath. "Are you ready for the third stage?"

She looked into his eyes. "How can I say no?"

"Holding hands!" Silas overturned his chair and grabbed his camera. The paper plate went flying into the sand. "Turn my back for one minute and look what happens."

He stalked toward the Jeep, snapping pictures with a vengeance.

"I should go, Jo Beth, before I make him too agitated."

"Colter . . ."

"Until tonight." He kissed her cheek, then vaulted on to his stallion and rode away.

Silas chased after him with the camera.

"Dad! Dad! Come back." Jo Beth caught up to him and took his arm. "It's all right, Dad. He's gone."

"Wait till Rick sees this evidence. He'll tar and feather that Toronto."

"I'm sure Rick will take care of everything." She patted his hand. "Now, why don't we load our gear and go back to the cabin. I'll bet Mom is lonesome without us."

"I'll take her picture."

"That's a grand idea."

Jo Beth loaded her equipment and the folding chair, then began to collect scraps. Sitting on the tailgate was Colter's burden basket. She picked it up and caressed its rough sides.

"Colter," she whispered. "What am I going to do?"

The call of the turtledove came late that night.

Jo Beth sat beside her open bedroom window and listened. Her parents had been in bed for at least two hours. They were safe, at least until morning.

She rose from the chair, and then sank back down, thinking. Could she do this? What if the impossible happened and she fell in love? Who in the world would watch after Silas and Sara?

The call of the turtledove sounded once more, urgently this time.

She leaned out the window. Colter was silhouetted by the moonlight, strong, bare-chested, and beautiful, astride the black stallion. She had to go. If she didn't, she'd always regret it.

Without another thought, she ran across the wooden floor and out the front door.

Colter saw her coming. Her hair was long and loose, and her feet were bare. When she reached the edge of the porch, she stopped. He urged the stallion to a gallop. The stallion veered sharply beside the porch, and Colter reached for her with his right arm. With one powerful motion, he swung her onto the blanket in front of him and raced off into the night.

They rode in silence. Colter was vividly aware of the woman in front of him, of her bright yellow hair, her pale white skin, and her slim hips, pressing against him. All his senses were alive. He felt the stirrings of the nocturnal desert creatures, saw the special brilliance of the heavens, and heard the soft rise and fall of Jo's breathing.

His arm tightened around her, and he pressed his knees into the stallion's sides, urging him on, hurrying him forward toward destiny. When his camp came into sight, he reined the stallion in.

He dismounted quickly and held his arms up to Jo. Her eyes were bright as she slid into them. He pressed her close for a moment, then released her.

"Wait by my side."

She stood quietly while he tethered the stallion and readied him for the night. Then he took her hand and led her into his tepee. A glimmer of moonlight shone through the smoke hole and around the loosely fitting door flap.

Jo Beth stood in the small shaft of light while her eyes adjusted to the semi-gloom of the tepee. When she saw Colter's blanket, spread upon the hard ground, she started toward it.

"No." He caught her shoulders. "Stand here where I can see you best."

Jo Beth trembled when he put his hands on her face.

"Are you afraid?" Colter stroked her cheeks.

"No. Excited."

His fingers traced her face, her eyebrows, her cheekbones, her nose, her lips. "You are beautiful."

"And you." Jo put one fingertip on his shoulder bone and raked it down his smooth bare chest.

When her finger met the resistance of his belt buckle, she traced the path back upward.

He caught her hand, pressing it flat against his skin. "You are so fair."

She kneaded her fingers in his warm flesh and closed her eyes. "Sometimes I think you must be a dream, Gray Wolf."

"Dreams can't do this." He kissed her. It was a joining of immense tenderness, and it took great restraint on his part. From the first day he'd met her, from the moment Jo Beth had followed him into the moonlight, he'd wanted her—here in his tepee, here in his arms. She was destined to be here, his gift from a capricious Fate. She belonged. She was his. And he would handle her the way he handled all precious gifts—with great care.

He lifted his head and gazed deeply into her eyes. "I want you here with me through the night."

"I'll stay until morning comes; then I must go."

"It will be time enough."

Still gazing into her eyes, he began to unbutton her blouse. She stood very still, watching the pleasure in his face as the blouse parted. He removed the blouse, folded it neatly, and placed it on a full duffel bag. He took the same care with the rest of her garments, handling them almost with reverence.

And when she stood before him, an alabaster carving save for the soft blush on her cheeks, he came to her. His hands and lips were poetry as they moved over her. She closed her eyes. The beauty of his touch filled her with fire until she was melting, her blood flowing richly through a body that was liquid and burning.

Suddenly she felt his hands leave her. There was a soft rustling in the tepee. Slowly, ever so slowly, she opened her eyes. "Colter?"

He was standing beside her, nude except for the bright Indian blanket draped over his shoulders. His eyes gleamed in a face gone tight with passion. He stretched out one arm and drew her to him. The heavy blanket fell around her.

They stood facing each other, shrouded in their bright cocoon. Her arms slid around his shoulders. He lifted her up and they became one.

A shaft of light pierced the velvety darkness, shining down on the two who loved. The blanket covered them, holding the heat, doubling the fire of their passion. Jo Beth clung to his shoulders, and Colter began to murmur in the musical language of his ancestors.

He lay down with her, the blanket spread underneath them. The rhythm of his Apache song increased with the rhythm of his body.

Jo Beth was carried to a place she'd never been, a bright and shining place, filled with light, rich with color, burning with the flames of a thousand stars. She climbed up, higher and higher, Earth Mother reaching for the Father Sky. The sky came down, bold, full of thunder and lightning. Earth trembled beneath it. Lightning seared, splitting the earth, burning through its core. The earth rocked with the assault; then slowly its fertile center opened to receive the life-giving rains of the sky.

Still joined, Jo Beth and Colter lay together on the blanket.

"What is that beautiful language you spoke?"

"Athabascan. The language of my people."

"Teach me." She traced her hands over his face.

"The language?" His smile was teasing.

"Whatever."

He sat up, taking her with him. Kneeling beside her, he taught her the words of simple courtesy, "please" and "thank you." He taught her words for greetings and partings.

"I need you, Yellow Bird."

"How do you say that?"

His eyes became hooded. "This is not a language lesson."

He reached for her. His hands were dark on her shoulders. He didn't bother with words; he didn't have to. His silence was more eloquent than a two-hour oration.

Her body went languid as he positioned her. He came to her kneeling. And the journey started all over again.

It was a journey that lasted through the night. And just before dawn pinked the sky, he dressed her and carried her from his tepee. The stallion neighed a soft greeting.

Colter put Jo Beth on the horse and mounted behind her. It was a different journey they made this time, a journey filled with the nostalgia of parting. Neither of them spoke until they were within sight of her cabin.

Leaning close to her ear, Colter whispered, "I'll come for you again tonight."

"Yes."

"Listen for my signal."

Then he lifted her off the stallion and watched until she had entered the cabin. She stood just inside the door, listening to the sound of hoofbeats until they faded in the distance.

Jo Beth had slept only three hours when her mother came to her bedroom door.

"I thought I'd better wake you, Jo Beth. You don't usually sleep this late."

"I guess I'm just tired from all the desert photography."

She hated lying. As she got out of bed she thought briefly about, confiding in her mother. Would Sara understand the need, the passion that had driven her to Colter's bed? Would she remember what it was like to want a man so badly that he filled her thoughts every waking moment? Jo Beth didn't know. Nor did she know how she would explain to Sara that Colter was more than an interlude, more than a desert affair, that he had toppled her beliefs and threatened her lifestyle in a way that no man ever had.

Instead of confiding, she smiled. "What would I do without the two of you taking care of me the way you do?" She reached for her robe. "Thanks, Mom."

Sara eyed her keenly. "Jo Beth, we both know who's the caretaker around here." She crossed the room and put her arm around her daughter's shoulders. "Honey, I don't want you sacrificing your life for us. We'll manage just fine."

"I know that, Mom. And I won't."

"Promise."

"I promise." Her fingers were crossed behind her back when she said it.

Jo Beth somehow managed to get her equipment loaded and out to a place where the giant saguaro cactus grew in abundance. For once, Silas was content to sit on the porch and read a book. It renewed her hope.

Alone in the desert, Jo Beth thought about Colter. Forget the sparks. He'd gone so far beyond sparks that he was setting dynamite next to her heart. She would have been thrilled to learn that love was not an obsolete art, except for one thing— her parents. She had two brothers to share the responsibility, but being a daughter was different. She felt a need to personally oversee their care. Rick had hired full-time help, of course. And they were good. There was no doubt about that. Rick's wife, Martha Ann, was more than willing to let Silas and Sara stay with them, but she had three rowdy boys who were more than a handful, all the same age, triplets. And she was pregnant again. Jo Beth couldn't ask her to take on more responsibility.

There was her brother, Andrew, of course, but he hardly had room for himself and his bird dogs at his little cabin in Boguefala Bottom. Anyhow, Andrew wasn't exactly the stabilizing influence Silas needed. He'd probably have Silas riding wild horses and chasing wild women.

Jo Beth wrapped up her day's work and headed back to the cabin. There was only one thing to do—break off with Colter before it was too late.

She didn't wait for the night; she drove straight to his camp. He came to the opening of his tepee. Jo Beth fought the urge to run straight to his arms, but she knew that if she went into that tepee, she wouldn't have the willpower to leave.

Hanging one arm over the side of the Jeep, she called, "I need to talk to you, Colter."

He walked toward her, his moccasins moving silently in the dust and his bare chest gleaming in the late-afternoon sun. He didn't speak until he was standing beside her Jeep.

"I'm listening, Jo Beth." He put one hand on her arm.

"Don't." She pulled her arm away. His face gave away nothing, neither surprise nor anger nor hurt. "I can't say what I have to say if you're touching me."

"Not touching you is pain, Yellow Bird."

"For me too." She looked at him standing beside her Jeep and was sorely tempted to change the nature of her visit. "I've been doing some thinking today, out in the desert by myself."

"It sounds serious."

"It is. First I want you to know that you've made me change my mind about falling in love."

He merely smiled, waiting.

"If there was ever a man I could fall in love with, Colter, it's you. I want to thank you for that."

"I liked the way you thanked me in the porch swing."

"So did I, but you don't have a porch swing." She tried to keep her voice teasing, but the tears kept showing through. Her throat was scratchy with emotion.

"Jo Beth, tell me what's wrong."

"You always know, don't you?"

"Only because it's you." He propped his arm on the Jeep and leaned toward her. "Tell me, Yellow Bird."

"This is not going to work." She made a sweeping gesture toward his tepee. "I can't turn my back on my responsibilities and ride off into the sunset with you . . . as much as I'd like to."

"There is never a problem that can't be solved with two good minds working together. We can work it out, Jo Beth."

"No. It's best this way—a quick, clean break." She turned the key, and the Jeep's engine roared to life.

"Jo Beth . . ."

"Don't come for me tonight, Colter." She stepped on the gas, and he jumped out of the way. The Jeep's tires stirred the dust as she backed quickly out of his camp and turned toward her cabin. She never looked back.

• • •

It was midnight when she heard the call of the turtledove.

She lay in her bed, willing him to go away. The call sounded once more. She balled her hands into fists and rammed them against her mouth to keep from crying out.

From the darkness came the third call, closer this time. The sound pierced her heart. She threw back the covers and ran from her bed, trailing bedspread and bed sheets across the wooden floor in her haste. She didn't even stop to think about clothes. All she knew was that she had to go to Colter.

He was waiting beside the porch when she came out. He didn't go directly to her but sat on his stallion, watching as she stood in the doorway, the moonlight shining through her filmy gown and gilding her with silver.

She lingered, waiting. He held out one hand, and she ran to him. One arm swung out and pulled her onto the stallion, then they raced away into the night.

She was aware of thundering hooves and a rhythmic rocking motion. Colter was an expert horseman. She leaned against him with complete trust. The rhythm changed and the stallion slowed down, almost to a halt.

"Turn, Jo Beth. Put your arm around my neck."

Automatically she obeyed. Colter lifted her and swung her around, astride his lap. She gasped. Her gown settled down around them, and Colter urged the stallion forward once more.

They rode through the night. With one arm around Jo Beth's waist and the other on the stallion's halter, Colter guided them both. The tepee rose up, large in the warm, dark night. And still they rode. All the rhythms of the earth seemed concentrated in the three of them—the stallion, the wild Gray Wolf, and his pretty Yellow Bird.

When they reached the stream in the foothills of the mountains, Colter brought them to a halt. Jo Beth leaned her head against his shoulder.

"I couldn't stay away, Jo Beth."

"And I couldn't refuse to come."

He brushed her damp hair back from her face and kissed her forehead. "We can work everything out."

He helped her from the stallion. She stood beside the stream, listening to the rushing sound of water while Colter tethered the horse. He came up behind her, circling his arms around her waist.

"Are you cold, Jo?"

"Not as long as I have you to keep me warm."

He pressed his face into her hair. "Do you want to talk?"

"Not yet." She leaned against him, taking comfort from the steady beat of his heart and the steady strength of his arms.

He cradled her, crooning a soft song in his native tongue.

"Warm me, Colter."

He led her to his blanket. There was no slow unveiling this time, but a haste made necessary by clamoring need. Theirs was a fierce joining, a coming together that sought to shut out the world. Their problems were forgotten in the frenzy of passion.

And when it was over, when they lay wrapped in a close embrace with only the moon to cover them, they talked.

"Tell me about your home, Jo. Do you live with your parents?"

"No. I have a small house across town from

them, and they have round-the-clock help, but I
don't like to depend on strangers for their care. I
take them on assignment whenever I can."

"There have been studies done of people like
your father. I know you take good care of him
and that nothing can take the place of a child's
love, but it has been proven that strict routine is
the best possible care."

She sat up. "Nursing homes?"

"Sometimes."

"Never. I will never send him off to one of those
places with cold tiles on the floor and indifferent
people behind their almighty desks, dispensing
false sympathy and big bills."

"I'm not suggesting that you should, at least
not yet. But when the time comes, I hope you'll
give the nursing homes a fair assessment. I think
you'll change your mind. There are many loving
and caring people out there who are also trained to
take care of people like Silas."

She stood up. "Take me back, Colter. This is no
solution, this is outrage."

"Jo. Hear me out." He reached for her, pulling
her back down. He cuddled her against his chest,
stroking her hair. "I'm trying to speak not as your
lover but as an objective professional."

"I don't need professional objectivity. He's my
father."

"I know that, Yellow Bird. I know that." He
rocked her in his arms a while, then reached for
his denim shirt. "Give me your arms, sweetheart."
He helped her into the shirt. While she fastened
the buttons, he pulled on his jeans.

She gave him a sheepish grin and went straight
to his arms.

"Sometimes when I don't get enough sleep I'm
mean and irrational."

"I have a cure." He smiled.

"Not yet." She pressed her forehead against his shoulder. "I'm ready to listen now."

"Jo Beth, the bottom line is that you are probably doing your father more harm than good by taking him with you everywhere you go. Strange places can be upsetting to people whose minds have a tenuous grasp on reality."

"Rick tried to tell me the same thing, but I wouldn't listen. He finally shut up and let me have my way."

"Rick didn't have as much at stake as I do. Let's lie down a while, Jo." Together they lay on the blanket.

"What you say makes sense, but still . . . I'd feel guilty leaving them with nobody but strangers all the time. And I can hardly take all my assignments in Tupelo." She sighed and closed her eyes.

"It's a matter of scheduling. You can live anywhere in the world, work anywhere in the world, and still schedule regular visits with your parents. And there's always the telephone. Sometimes telephone visits are just as uplifting as personal ones. . . . Jo?"

She was fast asleep. Colter covered her bare legs with his and gazed up at the stars.

How easy it was, he thought, to solve Jo's problems, and how hard it was to solve his own. He'd left the modern world behind and come to the desert in order to be alone, thinking that he could reconcile this division of loyalties, this division of his soul, in solitude. But Fate had sent him Jo Beth, the antithesis of everything Indian. Just as he had been on the brink of a decision to close his practice in San Francisco and go back to the reservation, his beautiful Yellow Bird had appeared. She was his chosen woman; he knew that. But could she ever fit into life on the reservation? Would she want to? And was that really what he wanted, to leave behind his friends, his practice, his city—and San Francisco had become his city. Was it possible for him to go home again? When Jo Beth's assignment here was finished, he would find out.

Jo awakened to the sound of water splashing. She opened her eyes and found herself staring at a pale gray sky. For a moment she was disoriented, and then she smiled. Turning her head toward the sound, she saw Colter, bathing in the stream.

He smiled at her. "It will soon be morning, Jo." He held out his hand.

She shed his denim shirt and joined him. The water was cool, and she shivered.

He came to her and wrapped her in his arms. "Need someone to keep you warm?"

"Is that an offer?"

"One you can't refuse."

He lifted her up, and they stood in the middle of the swirling stream, saying good morning and good-bye at the same time. Then they finished their bath, dressed, and rode away toward Jo Beth's cabin.

The morning sun was decorating the sky when he helped her off the stallion and onto her front porch. He leaned down for one last kiss.

"I must hurry," she said softly.

"Listen for my call, Yellow Bird."

He wheeled away and headed across the desert. Jo slipped inside to bed.

Six

Their routine held for six more days—the call of the turtledove, the ride through the night to his tepee, the return to her cabin just before morning came.

On the sixth night she rose from his blanket and stood in the opening of his tepee, looking out across the desert.

"I finished my assignment today, Colter. I'll be leaving."

"I thought you might." He came and stood behind her. "Lean on me, Jo."

She rested her back against him. He buried his face in her pale hair. They stood that way for a while, and then Colter spoke.

"I want you to go with me."

"Where?"

"Into the White Mountains to meet my family." He kissed the top of her head. "I'm not asking for commitment. At least not yet. I want you to see my home, to know my background, to understand who I am."

She turned to face him. "Colter, did you find what you were looking for out here in the desert?"

"Only you, Jo. I found only you."

She leaned her back against him once more, drawing his arms around her waist. "I'll go with you, Colter. Give me time to make arrangements for my parents."

"I'll help you."

Later that morning, after she had talked to her parents, she and Colter went into Tucson. She drove the rented Jeep and he drove his borrowed truck, pulling the horse trailer behind him. While he returned the truck and the stallion and made arrangements for their trip, she placed a call to Tupelo.

After six rings, she gave up on Rick and called Andrew. He answered on the first ring. She could hear his bird dogs howling in the background.

"Andrew, can you hear me?"

"Is that you, Jo Beth? Can you speak up?"

"I'm staying in Arizona a while longer. Can you meet Mom and Dad at the airport?"

"You're flying in? When?"

"No. *They're* flying in. Can you pick them up and get them settled into their house? They are both eager to come home."

"I'll not only see them safely settled, I'll take them out on the town. A welcome-home party. Heck, I might even invite two or three buddies of mine. We could get a keg—"

"Andrew." She rolled her eyes heavenward.

"What?"

"Just pick them up and forget the party. Can I trust you?"

"What kind of question is that to ask your one and only, most sought-after bachelor brother in the entire state? I'm as trustworthy as the First Mutual Bank, and a heck of a lot better looking."

"You're a clown too. Thanks, Andrew."

By ten o'clock the next day, Silas and Sara were on a plane going home, while Colter, Jo Beth, and Zar headed north into the White Mountains. Colter had rented something larger and more substantial than her Jeep—a Dodge Ram Charger with plenty of room for her equipment and his supplies.

It took them three hours to reach his Apache home. Colter was strangely quiet during their journey. Jo Beth was accustomed to his watchful silences, but this quietness was different. It was disturbing rather than tranquil. Apprehension pricked at her nerves and caught at her heart.

She tried to initiate several conversations, but each one died for lack of adequate response. Finally she contented herself with alternately watching Colter and the scenery.

They crossed the Salt River. The reservation lay just north, more than a million acres of beautiful mountain country.

Suddenly Colter pulled the truck off the steep mountain road and parked. He and Jo Beth stood on a lookout point that allowed them a panoramic view of the vast land. She turned from the view to watch his face. It gave away nothing.

"How long since you've been here, Colter?"

"Too long." He studied the mountains in silence, then added, "Three years, Jo Beth. Except for Mother, who makes the trek to San Francisco once a year, I haven't seen my family nor the land of Tin-ne-ah for three years."

"Tin-ne-ah?"

"The People. That's what we usually call ourselves. Apache was a name given to us by others." He held out his hand. "Come."

They drove thirty minutes more before his mother's house came into sight. Jo leaned forward. She didn't know what she had expected, but not the neat white frame house snuggled between tall pines. There was even a white picket fence and a mailbox, painted blue, that proclaimed *Patricia Gray Lives Here.* To the west, in a paddock as well ordered as any that handled Kentucky racing stock, a magnificent white stallion and three sorrel mares romped.

Colter parked the truck, then held out his hand to Jo Beth.

"Are you ready, Jo?"

"I'm a little nervous. Do you think your mother will like me?"

"When she gets to know you, I believe she will love you. But don't expect too much. The Apaches don't show much emotion."

"I could argue with that."

He smiled. "Only in certain circumstances."

Jo Beth took his hand, and together they climbed from the truck.

Patricia Gray, known as Little Deer to everyone except the mailman, saw them coming. She'd been watching from the window for two hours, eager to see the friend Colter had said he was bringing home. She smiled when her tall son emerged from the fancy truck. Nothing but the best for her Gray Wolf, she thought.

Her smile froze when she saw his friend, a slender woman with hair the color of jonquils and skin like milk. She put her hand over her heart and eased into her chair. That Colter could do such a thing to her in her old age was astonishing. She rocked back and forth, muttering to herself. She'd not look. When they came in, she'd pretend she had forgotten they were coming.

Curiosity got the best of her. She parted the curtain and peered out the window again. They were holding hands. Her son was going to send her to an early grave.

She leaned her head back in her chair and closed her eyes. Maybe she was having a heart attack. Maybe she was going to the Spirit World at that very moment, even as her son, who could have been the greatest shaman on the reservation, was coming through the door.

"Mother."

She kept her eyes closed, leaned her head back, and began to rock, very fast. The rocker was old and creaky and not accustomed to such punishment, but she didn't care. Perhaps it would fall into splinters, and she'd die there on her freshly swept floor, right in front of their eyes.

"Mother." She could feel them both standing by her chair. "Are you ill, Mother?"

"I'm feeling faint. I guess it's the shock." She opened her eyes and looked directly at the yellow-haired woman.

Colter's hand tightened on Jo Beth's. He'd expected surprise and even resistance, but he'd never expected such an outrageous reaction from his mother.

He bent down and felt her pulse. It was as steady and reliable as the old clock on the mantle. He straightened back up. He wasn't going to coddle her.

"Mother." He made his voice sharp enough so that she would know he meant business. "I want you to meet my friend, Jo Beth McGill."

Little Deer gave the woman a cunning smile, and then she began to speak in rapid Athabascan. She complimented the stranger her son had brought home on her pale hair, her pale skin, and her pale eyes. Finally, she had to pause for breath.

"Jo Beth, Mother welcomes you to our home." Colter's face didn't register his anger. "Mother, speak English, please. Our guest does not understand Athabascan."

Little Deer got up from her chair. "I will show our guest her room. She must be tired from the trip."

"Thank you, Mrs. Gray. I would like to store my things."

Little Deer smiled with satisfaction. The woman was foolish. Nobody but the mailman called her Mrs. Gray.

"Follow me." She led Jo Beth from the room while Colter went to get their belongings.

Her house was L-shaped, with two bedrooms in the east wing and two on the far north. Colter and his brother had occupied the east rooms, while she and her husband had occupied the two on the north. Since she was the only one left in the house, with Gray Fox long since dead and both her sons gone, she kept the north wing all to herself and let guests use the east bedrooms.

She made a quick change of plans. "Miss McGill, I hope you find this room satisfactory." Little Deer discreetly knocked a cobweb off the dresser as she walked by. "I think you'll enjoy this northern exposure. My room is right next door, in case you need anything."

"That's very kind of you."

When Colter's mother didn't reply, Jo Beth stood uncertainly in the doorway. She didn't know what to say to this strange woman. She wanted to put her arms around her and say, "I love your son and I want to love you too." But she sensed Mrs. Gray's resistance. The situation called for patience, a virtue she didn't possess. She supposed she'd have to learn from Colter.

She entered the room. "There is a lovely view from the window."

Mrs. Gray remained silent. Jo Beth tried again. "Colter said it was all right to bring my dog. I hope you don't mind."

Again, silence. Jo Beth was desperately searching for something else to say when Colter appeared in the doorway with her bags. She'd never been so happy to see a person in all her life.

"Of course she doesn't mind. Do you, Mother?" He glanced at his mother as he came into the room and stowed Jo Beth's bags.

"If my son says the dog is welcome, he is welcome." Little Deer sat down in a chair beside the bed and folded her hands.

Colter knew exactly what his mother was doing. She had instantly labeled Jo Beth an outsider, unsuitable for her son, and had deliberately made her inaccessible to him in the house. Now she was watching them both with her eagle eyes to make sure Jo Beth didn't work love magic on him. If he had been the grinning kind, he would have grinned. What his mother didn't know was that Jo had already worked love magic on him.

Coming home again was going to be hard, and coming home with Jo Beth even harder. He crossed the room and put his arm around Jo Beth's waist. She was stiff with tension.

"Why we go into the kitchen and all have a cup of tea?" he said.

"I don't serve company in the kitchen. I will serve in the den." Little Deer got up and shuffled slowly across the room.

"Have you developed arthritis, Mother?"

"It's the agony of life." His mother looked at Jo Beth, then turned and left the room.

"I don't think she likes me," Jo Beth whispered.

"She'll come around." Colter squeezed her waist. "The important thing is that *I* like you."

Jo Beth smiled at him, and they followed his mother into the den.

Little Deer sat on a small sofa and patted the seat. "Come, my son. Sit beside me. We haven't seen each other for too long."

Colter knew what she was up to, but in order to keep peace, he sat on the two-seater beside her. Jo Beth took a chair opposite them.

"You look good, my son. How have you been in that heathen city?"

"I wish you would visit more often and see for yourself, Mother. Remember the ballet you loved so well? The *Nutcracker Suite*? It will be playing again soon."

Little Deer started to smile, then remembered herself. "The ballet is a silly dance with no purpose." She stood up. "I'll bring the tea."

"Can I help you, Mrs. Gray?"

"I don't allow strangers in my kitchen." Holding herself straight and tall, she hurried out.

"I guess she forgot about the agony of life." The minute the words were out of her mouth, Jo Beth wanted to call them back. "I'm sorry, Colter. I shouldn't have said that."

Colter couldn't hold back a chuckle. He got up, took Jo Beth's hands, and guided her back across the room to the two-seater.

"You're doing very well under the circumstances." When they were seated, he put his arm across her shoulders. "After the tea, I'll take you outside to show you the ranch."

Little Deer came through the door with the tea. When she saw who occupied her seat, she set the tea tray down with a bang on the coffee table.

"I didn't mean to take so long with the tea."

"Mother, you were so fast I suspect you of harboring elves in the kitchen to help out." Colter poured the tea.

"What is this? Elves?" She pulled a chair up so close to the sofa it nearly banged against Colter's leg; then she turned her attention to Jo Beth. "This son of mine—he could have been the greatest shaman on the reservation, a diyin of such power his people would have come from many miles to seek his help. He could have had many horses and a fine black-eyed wife, and what does he do? He goes off to that heathen city and comes back talking about elves. There have been witches at work."

"I don't believe in witches, Mrs. Gray." Jo Beth sipped her tea.

Little Deer gave her a sly smile. "Love witches are the strongest. They cast their spells when a man is not looking."

Jo Beth stiffened. While she was trying to think of how to reply to being labeled a love witch, Colter intervened.

"Jo Beth is right. There are no unexplainable phenomena in this modern age except the miracles of our Father Creator." Colter set his and Jo Beth's half-empty cups on the tray. Then he stood up, taking her with him. Facing his mother, he put his arm around Jo Beth in an unmistakable gesture of possession. "I'm going to show Jo Beth the ranch. The tea was refreshing, Mother."

Colter didn't hurry from the room. He'd made his statement and he knew that Little Deer would respect that, at least for a while.

The stiffness was still apparent in Jo Beth. He felt a great urge to comfort her, to assure her that everything would work out. But just when he needed the words most, they seemed to have van-

ished. In the open spaces of the desert with none
to hear him except Yellow Bird and the wind, he
had been poetic. But now, with the ghosts of his
ancestors whispering in his ear, with ancient memories stirring in his mind, he felt a strange
restraint.

There was only one way he could comfort her,
and in that area he felt no constraint at all. If
anything, having Jo Beth in the land of his people
heightened his passion.

The door closed behind them, and they stepped
out into the cool mountain air.

"Thank you for rescuing me back there, Colter."

"I will always rescue you, Jo." He gazed down
into her face. What he wanted to say was *I will
always love you*, but he couldn't. How could he
speak of a future with her when he didn't know
what the future held for him?

"Thank you, Colter." She put her hand on the
side of his cheek. What she wanted to say was
Hold me, Colter. Never let me go. But she felt the
barriers between them. Since they'd arrived on
this mountain, she'd had the uneasy feeling that
she was losing Colter. If she'd known what she
was losing him to, she could have fought. But not
knowing, she was helpless.

"I'm glad you came with me, Yellow Bird." He
slid his hands into her hair, reveling in the familiar silkiness. What he meant to say was *I can
never forget the feel of your hair*, but the poetry
seemed to have vanished from his soul.

"Why did you bring me here, Colter?" When he
started to speak, she put her hand over his lips. "I
know what you told me in the desert, that you
wanted me to know and understand you. But I
already do. I learned you in the desert." She started
to add *And I love what you are*, but she sensed

that the time was not right. Saying those words now was impossible.

"I brought you because you are my woman."

She gazed into his face, trying to read him. But that, too, was impossible. "Show me your home, Colter.'"

"I will show you many things."

He took her hand and hurried with her toward the paddock. The white stallion lifted his head and whinnied. When they reached the fence, Colter called to the horse. The animal shook his head once, twice, and then galloped toward them.

"That's remarkable." Jo Beth leaned over the railing, watching the stallion run. "You haven't been here in three years, and yet he acts as if he knows you."

"An animal never forgets his master."

"He's yours?"

"Yes." The stallion had reached the fence. Colter rubbed the soft muzzle. "I bought Chieftain six years ago when he was a colt. I trained him here in the mountains. And when he grew old enough to want companions, I bought him three lovely ladies." He gestured toward the sorrel mares, tossing their heads and watching the white stallion.

"I think they're jealous."

"Probably. They're used to having him to themselves."

He opened the gate and let the white stallion through. Chieftain followed them to the barn. Colter got a colorful blanket and spread it on the stallion's back. Then he mounted and swung Jo Beth up in front of him.

She laughed when she'd settled onto the blanket. "I'm getting good at this."

"You make a good Apache, Yellow Bird."

He spoke softly to the stallion, and Chieftain

cantered across the open pastures behind the barn
and into the sparse trees. As they climbed higher
and higher, the trees became denser, greener. Tow-
ering pines spread their branches over the trio,
shrouding them in cool green solitude.

The forest became so dense that the late-evening
sun could barely reach through to touch them.
And still they climbed. Suddenly they came upon
a bower, a small open space surrounded by thick
growth and padded with lush moss.

Colter pulled the stallion to a halt, then dismounted and held his arms up to Jo. She slid
into them. Without a word, Colter captured her
lips. It was an all-consuming kiss of such intensity that Jo had to cling to him to keep her knees
from buckling.

Chieftain nudged Colter's back and, getting no
response, trotted a few feet away to stand waiting.
Colter was only vaguely aware that the stallion
had not forgotten his training.

He lifted Jo and carried her into the bower.

"Colter . . ."

"Shhh."

His hands were on her buttons almost before
her feet touched the ground. She heard a small
tearing as one stubborn button refused to be ma-
nipulated in haste. She stood very still while he
tore and threw aside her clothes. It was a Colter
she had never seen, a savage man, wild with need
and desire.

She welcomed this new facet of him. She wanted
to know Colter in all his moods and ways. When
their clothes were cast aside and he had pressed
her down upon the moss, she greeted him with a
fire to match his own.

The tiny fingers of sun across their skin changed
from gold to pink to red. A pair of wings stirred in

the branches above their heads and a pair of yellow eyes looked down upon them. As the forest readied itself for evening, it murmured and rustled. Brave nighttime creatures came up from their burrows and timid daytime creatures sought the shelter of their homes.

Gray Wolf loved his Yellow Bird. He sought with his body to tell her all the things he couldn't put into words. He told her in eloquent, age-old ways to be patient with him, to understand him, and above all, to love him. In the language of love, he promised to care for her, to keep her, to protect her, to understand her, and to cherish her.

When they lay still in each other's arms, she stroked his hair. "It's beautiful here, Colter."

"I'm glad you like it."

"I love it. I'll always remember this place. Colter, why did you stop coming here three years ago?"

"It's a part of my past I cannot share."

He pulled her to her feet, and Jo regretted asking him. If she hadn't, he might have been content to stay in that lovely spot a while longer. But not now. He dressed in haste, and she saw yet another side of him, a restless man, driven by private demons.

Colter whistled for his horse, and when he started to mount, Jo Beth caught his hand.

"Love me enough to trust me, Colter."

"I trust you, Jo."

"Then talk to me." She caught the front of his shirt. "In the desert you helped me with my problems. Let me help you with yours."

"Yellow Bird . . ." He touched her face, and for a moment she thought he was going to confide in her. Instead, he turned and mounted the stallion. Holding out his hand, he said, "Come."

She hesitated only a second, then took his hand and allowed herself to be lifted up. They rode back down the mountain in silence.

Colter's mother had dinner waiting. While they had been gone, she'd apparently decided to behave herself. She was not only pleasant, but she even made a few attempts to be friendly. Jo Beth was grateful for small favors. After what had happened in the forest, she didn't think she could have handled a silent Colter *and* a hostile hostess.

"I saw your cameras when Colter brought your things in. Do you like making pictures?"

She still didn't call Jo Beth by her name, but her friendly overture was a start. Jo Beth smiled at her.

"I've loved it since I was ten years old. That's when Dad bought me my first camera."

"Since you're here, you might want to make my picture."

"I'd be delighted to do that, Mrs. Gray. Thank you."

Colter watched them, smiling. Everything was going to be all right, he thought. Everything would work out.

After dinner, Jo Beth got her camera while Little Deer cleaned the dishes. She had still refused to allow Jo Beth in her kitchen. This time, however, she'd been polite enough not to call her son's friend a stranger.

Little Deer came into the den, and she was like a child when she saw the camera. She had to touch it and admire it. Then she asked dozens of questions about it.

When she had satisfied her curiosity, she sat in her rocking chair and announced, "I'm ready for my picture now." She immediately struck a stiff pose.

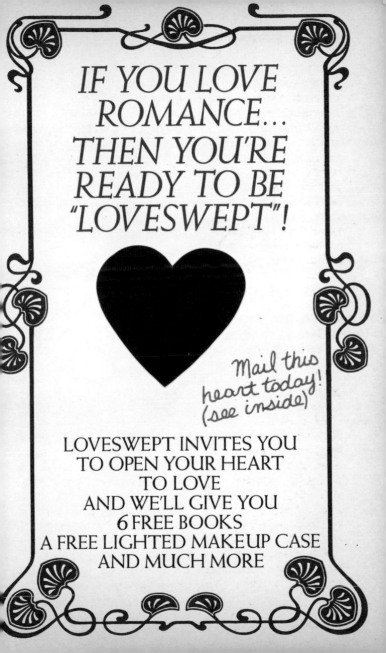

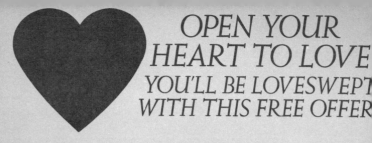
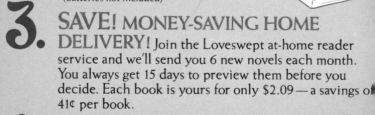

FREE–LIGHTED MAKEUP CASE!
FREE–6 LOVESWEPT NOVELS!

- NO OBLIGATION
- NO PURCHASE NECESSARY

(DETACH AND MAIL CARD TODAY.)

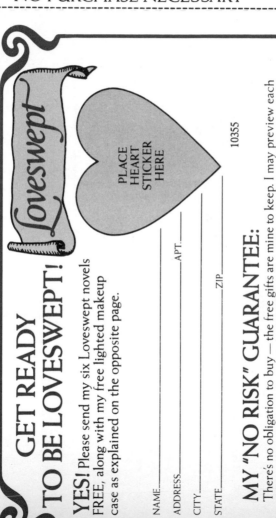

GET READY TO BE LOVESWEPT!

YES! Please send my six Loveswept novels FREE, along with my free lighted makeup case as explained on the opposite page.

PLACE HEART STICKER HERE

10355

NAME_____

ADDRESS_____ APT._____

CITY_____

STATE_____ ZIP._____

MY "NO RISK" GUARANTEE:

There's no obligation to buy — the free gifts are mine to keep. I may preview each subsequent shipment for 15 days. If I don't want it, I simply return the books within 15 days and owe nothing. If I keep them I will pay just $12.50 (I save $2.50 off the retail price for 6 books) plus postage and handling and any applicable sales tax.

BRjfm

Prices subject to change. Orders subject to approval.

REMEMBER!

- The free books and gift are mine to keep!
- There is no obligation!
- I may preview each shipment for 15 days!
- I can cancel anytime!

"I really would prefer to get candid shots, Mrs. Gray. Just try to act as if the camera is not here."

"How can I do that? I can see it."

"Perhaps if you don't look at it, I can capture that natural animation you have."

"You think I have natural animation? Well, how about this?" She bared her teeth in a grimace that made her look as if she were suffering lower back pain.

Colter chuckled. "Mother, just pretend you are talking to Bessie Running Water on the telephone. I've never seen more natural animation than that."

She turned to her son. "Oh, go away, you clever-talking Gray Wolf. You tell a mother's secrets."

While the two of them were talking, Jo Beth's camera clicked. She got three good shots before Mrs. Gray started posing again.

They spent the rest of the evening with Jo Beth taking pictures. Finally, Little Deer rose from her chair.

"It's time for bed." She took Jo Beth's hand. "Come, my dear. You must be tired from all that work and the long drive today."

Her ploy was so obvious that Jo Beth found it hard to keep from laughing. Colter, who was leaning against the mantel, intervened.

"I'm sure Jo can find her way down the hall."

"I will not leave a tired guest standing around while I go to bed and sleep like a buffalo."

Colter started to protest again, but Jo spoke up.

"I *am* a little tired. Good night, Colter."

"Good night, Yellow Bird."

He watched while his mother led Jo Beth into the north wing. Then he left the house and walked out into the night, hoping to find answers in the solitude of the dark mountains.

• • •

The sound came out of the darkness, soft and muted.

Jo Beth snuggled deeper into her pillows. The sound came again—the call of the turtledove. She'd been in bed for what must have been hours. She decided she was dreaming. Rolling over to get more comfortable, she hit a solid object. Her eyes flew open.

"Colter."

"Shhh." He was sitting on the side of her bed.

"How on earth . . ." she whispered, sitting up. "I didn't hear you come in."

"Did you think I'd fail to come for you? You are as necessary to me as breathing."

He threw back the sheet and lifted her from the bed. She kissed the side of his neck as he glided silently from the room.

"Where are you taking me?"

"Does it matter?"

"No. As long as we're together."

Seven

Jo Beth sat up in Colter's bed. Instinct must have awakened her, for she remembered hearing no sound.

Colter was standing beside the dark window, his face in profile. The muscles along his back were knotted with tension and his face was pensive. There was nothing to see out the window except blackness, so she knew he was looking inward.

A sudden chill of fear seized her. She called to him softly, "Colter."

"It's almost morning, Jo."

She got up and padded barefoot across the floor. Wrapping her arms around his waist, she snuggled her face against his back.

"What do you see out there?"

"Ghosts."

She smiled. "First your mother's witches and now your ghosts. If this mountain if so filled with spooks, perhaps I should leave."

"Ghosts of the past, Jo."

"Tell me about them."

He didn't reply, but stood with his face turned to the darkened window. Jo pressed her lips into his back. He shivered.

"Talk to me, Colter."

His muscles tightened, then slowly relaxed. He reached behind with one arm and pulled her around to face him. He rubbed the back of his hand along her cheek.

"I love waking up with you at my side. Have I ever told you that?"

"Yes. In the desert. But I'm greedy. I'd like to hear it a million times."

"If I do all that I won't have time for this." He bent and captured her lips.

"Hmmm . . ." Ghosts were temporarily forgotten as she savored the sweetness of his kiss. Then she remembered his face, and the fear came over her again. "Colter . . ."

"Jo . . ." His lips skimmed down the side of her neck. "Don't talk."

"You're sidetracking me."

"If we talk, we won't have time for this." He picked her up and carried her back to bed.

"It's getting late."

"We have a little while until morning comes."

She lifted her arms and pulled him down to her.

Later that morning Jo Beth stood on the cracked sidewalk of the small village five miles from Colter's house, watching while he prepared for the footrace. A game day had been organized in his honor, and people had come from miles around to participate.

Stripped to the waist and dressed in jeans and moccasins, he crouched at the starting line, waiting for the footrace to begin. She wanted to reach out and pluck him away from the race, away from this haunted mountain. He blended in so well with these strange surroundings that she was afraid they would swallow him up and she'd never see him again.

Why won't you confide in me? she wanted to scream. Instead she rammed her hands into her jeans pockets and tried to be a part of the crowd. But that was impossible. They were beautifully, proudly Indian. And while they were polite to her, they were not openly friendly. Colter had said it was their way, but still, she felt like an outsider— except at night, except in Colter's arms.

She shifted to get a better view of Colter. Her slight movement caused Zar to push against her legs and whine. She bent over and patted his head.

The signal was given and the runners were off. Jo Beth watched Colter. He was a superb athlete— lithe, quick, powerful. He won the race with ease, and she whooped and cheered.

The crowd around her clapped politely, and a few gave her curious looks. She squatted beside her dog, patting his head.

"I've done it again, Zar."

"Done what, Yellow Bird?"

She hadn't heard Colter come up beside her. He was standing with the sun at his back, smiling down at her.

"Given proof that I'm not Apache."

"You don't have to be Apache, Jo. Be yourself."

"Thank you, Colter." Standing up, she touched his face. "You were beautiful out there. I'm so proud of you."

"A man likes to impress his chosen woman."

"I'm impressed." She linked her arm through his. "These games are interesting. What's next?"

"A stave game for the women, hoop and pole for the men."

"I'd much prefer to play hoop and pole with you."

"These are ancient games, Jo Beth. On these game days we still do everything in the traditional way in order to keep our culture alive. Women are not permitted to play hoop and pole."

"Then I'll watch and cheer you on."

"I'm sorry. That's impossible."

"Why?"

"It is taboo."

She started to protest, then changed her mind. Colter traced one hand down her cheek.

"Let's skip the games a while, Jo Beth. We'll walk down to my brother's store and get ice cream."

He nodded toward the building on the west side of the grassy square.

"No, Colter. That would be running away, and that's not fair to you."

"Running away from what, Jo? The games? We'll hardly be missed, and I certainly won't miss them."

"It's not the games. It's this Apache tradition. You came back to your people to find something, and I can't take you away from that."

"You are very wise, my Yellow Bird."

"If I'm so wise, why don't you trust me?"

"I do."

"Then please talk to me."

He smiled. "There's a good bawdy myth I could tell you, or would you prefer some erotic Apache poetry?"

"Be serious, Colter. You know what I'm talking about. *Confide* in me."

He gazed down at her, but he wasn't seeing or hearing a lively blond woman; he was looking inward, seeing and hearing a dying old man, his face as white as the pillow he lay upon, his voice raspy. "Promise me, Gray Wolf. Promise me. . . ."

He shook his head to rid himself of the voice.

"It's a journey of the soul, Jo. I have to make it alone."

She felt the cold winds of doubt and fear blow over her. In the desert their love had been perfect. Isolated from the real world they had laughed and loved and lived in almost perfect understanding and harmony. But here in these distant and forbidding mountains, Colter was pulling away from her, disappearing into a silence that she couldn't penetrate, an isolation she couldn't understand.

"Go play your game, Colter." She pulled away from him and whistled to her dog.

"Jo . . ." Colter lifted his hand in the gesture that was so familiar, the entreaty that she had never ignored, never until today.

"Don't say it. Don't say *come*, because I'm too weak to refuse you."

He hesitated, torn between wanting to stay and clear up the misunderstanding with her and wanting to go and enter once more into the games of his people.

"I'll go . . . for now." He traced the curve of her lips with one finger. "Wait for me, Jo. Please." Then he turned and walked away.

Jo Beth watched until he had disappeared around the corner of the village's only gas station, an aging frame building that tilted heavily to one side and looked as if a stiff wind would topple it over. Then she searched the crowd for Colter's mother.

Little Deer saw her oldest son heading for the ball field where hoop and pole would be played, leaving behind the fair-skinned woman he'd brought to the White Mountains. At first she was filled with glee, and then she saw the dejected slump of the woman's shoulders. She closed her eyes and pretended not to see, but she remembered the camera and how much she liked having her picture made. More than that, she remembered how fiercely her son had protected the woman.

She turned to her friend, Bessie Running Water. "Gray Wolf has left his friend alone."

"You should be glad. Didn't you tell me she is a used woman?"

Little Deer hesitated. She had heard the noises in the night—Gray Wolf coming to fetch the woman. She didn't know why she had ever told such a thing to Bessie Running Water, the biggest mouth in the village. It was one thing to talk about a used woman, but it was another thing to talk about her son.

"My son is perfect. He would never fool with a used woman."

"You told me she was used."

"You need a hearing aid, Bessie Running Water. I told you she was a *news* woman. She makes pictures for magazines."

"She makes pictures?" Bessie plumped up her hair and sucked in her fat stomach. "Do you think she might make a picture of me?"

"No. I'm the one who poses for her. Go play the stave game. I must go to the woman Gray Wolf goes about with."

Little Deer left the table where lunch was being prepared and went to Jo Beth.

"I saw you standing alone."

Jo Beth smiled. "I was looking for you."

"Did you want to make another picture? You could drive us home to get the camera."

"Do you mind if we wait until tonight? I'd like

to stay here and wait for Colter. When we go home to dress for the dance, I'll get my camera."

"Then come with me. I will show you the village."

Jo Beth and Little Deer walked down the cracked sidewalks toward her youngest son's general store. On the way she pointed out the coffee shop, the gas station, and the dentist's office, giving a running commentary on each. She was a good historian, and Jo Beth enjoyed the tour.

"What is that building over there, Mrs. Gray?"

"The beauty shop. Bessie Running Water's daughter runs it. It took us ten years to convince her to share her beauty secrets."

"That's nice. But I'm talking about the unfinished building next to it."

"That's Gray Wolf's clinic."

"His clinic?"

Jo Beth stood in amazement, looking at the concrete slab and the steel girders grown over with vines.

"He has not told you of this clinic?"

"No. I'd like to know its history."

"It is for Gray Wolf to say."

Little Deer clamped her mouth shut, and Jo Beth faced another wall of silence. She was disturbed but not defeated. She put her hand on Little Deer's arm.

"I'm trying to understand your son, Mrs. Gray. I love him."

Little Deer studied Jo Beth's face, and suddenly she saw the truth. This woman truly loved her son . . . and he loved her. True love was so rare that it had to be guarded and protected. And if it broke her heart for a little while that her oldest son's wife would be a pale woman with yellow hair, she'd get over it when the babies started coming, for she knew that Gray Wolf was a powerful diyin. All the babies would look like him.

Little Deer smiled and covered the pale hand with her own. "I believe you do, my child. And you may call me Little Deer."

Jo Beth was relieved and happy over Little Deer's sign of acceptance. "Little Deer, about this clinic—" Zar's frantic barking interrupted Jo Beth. "Where is my dog?" She looked around for Zar, and the barking sounded again from the direction Colter had gone. "It's over there. He must have followed Colter." She sprinted off.

"Come back," Little Deer called. "Women are taboo."

She kept on running. She passed the row of stores, rounded the dilapidated service station, and came suddenly upon a small, grassy ball field. It was in chaos. Men in fringed buckskins were running this way and that, yelling and chasing after a gleeful golden retriever who had stolen the hoop. They were no match for Zar. He bounded ahead of them. Occasionally he dropped his prize, waved his tail in the air, and gave his you-can't-catch-me bark.

Jo Beth laughed and joined the chase. "Zar," she called. "Drop it, boy. You're ruining the game."

Twenty-five Indians came to a dead halt. Twenty-five pairs of eyes stared at her. Jo Beth kept running toward her mischievous dog. Colter watched, aware of the consequences, torn between going after Jo Beth and staying to placate his friends.

Suddenly the astonished hoop-and-pole players went into action, milling and talking.

"It's a woman," someone yelled.

"Taboo! Taboo!"

"It's Gray Wolf's woman."

"Go after her."

Colter's decision was made. He held up one hand. "Stop." He didn't speak loudly; he didn't have to.

Standing head and shoulders taller than the rest of them and with a face as fierce as the animal he'd been named for, he commanded their attention. "She is my woman. No one touches her."

Still laughing, Jo Beth had reached Zar. When she heard Colter's voice, her laughter died. Too late, she realized that she had violated a sacred rule. With one hand on Zar's collar, she turned to watch the group of men. Some of them were having a hard time keeping from laughing, but many of them, particularly the older ones, were obviously disturbed. And Colter was facing them.

A stocky man of about thirty stepped forward. "You know the rules, Gray Wolf."

"Yes. I know the rules. But Jo Beth does not. Neither does her dog. How do you expect a twentieth-century golden retriever to know he's a descendant of the legendary coyote?" He smiled at them.

His attempt to use humor to lighten the situation worked. Several men chuckled. One agreed with him.

"Gray Wolf is right. Anyhow, it's only a game. An old game, as a matter of fact. I'd much rather be home watching baseball on TV."

But others were not so easily satisfied. "If all our women and their dogs violated the rules, there would be no tradition."

"Tradition is a valuable part of our culture and should be preserved," Colter said, "but not at the expense of common sense and common courtesy."

He left the group and walked toward Jo Beth. When he reached her, he put his arm around her shoulders.

"I didn't mean to cause trouble, Colter."

"You didn't. As a matter of fact, this game hasn't been so much fun since Bessie Running Water's cat crossed the field and got his tail caught in the hoop." He chuckled. "You should have seen the look on Big Elk's face when Zar stole the hoop. I thought the whole thing was funny."

"You're just saying that to make me feel better."

"Does it?"

"Yes." She laughed.

"That's what I love to hear—the sound of your laughter." He tipped her face up with one finger. "Do you want to stay and watch the game?"

"You'd do that? After defending me, don't you think flaunting me would be too much?"

"On second thought, it might give some of the younger men ideas." He smiled at her. "And I don't want any other man having ideas about you."

"Because I am your woman?" she asked lightly.

"Yes. Because you are my woman."

Together they left the playing field, with Zar trotting along behind them. They joined Colter's mother at the dinner table, and for the first time since Jo Beth had arrived, the three of them had a lively conversation. Jo Beth considered it a milestone.

She tasted all the native foods that had been prepared—the pit-baked mescal, the boiled locust tree blossoms, the cactus fruits. And she watched Colter.

The dinner tables had been set up under a grove of trees across the square from his unfinished clinic. From time to time he glanced in that direction. Sometimes he looked quickly away, and other times he stared.

It was during one of those long gazes that she spoke to him. "That's your clinic, isn't it?"

He turned to her, but his face showed neither surprise nor anger. "How did you know?"

"Your mother and I toured the village. I asked her about that building. Why didn't you finish it?"

His eyes darkened, and she saw the pain there. She reached out and squeezed his hand.

"It hurts, doesn't it, Colter?"

"Yellow Bird . . ." he lifted her hand to his lips and kissed it. His eyes cleared, and for a moment she thought he was going to tell her about his clinic. Instead, he laughed. "Why spoil a perfect day talking about things that don't matter anymore?"

"Is it a perfect day?"

"It is, and it will continue to be. There's the cross-country race this afternoon—which I will win. And you will be at the finish line to greet me, dressed in your prettiest party dress. Then we will dance the night away . . . unless you have better ideas."

She could only guess how much of his good humor and optimism was make-believe. But how could she be afraid when he was there at her side?

After the meal the four of them drove back home, Colter and Jo Beth in the front seat and Little Deer in the back seat with Zar. Jo Beth had insisted that Little Deer ride up front with Colter, but Little Deer had been just as adamant about leaving that seat of honor for Jo Beth.

"Contrary to what you might think, I know how to act in these situations."

Neither Colter nor Jo Beth had dared ask her, "What situations;" they were too busy counting their blessings. When they reached home, Little Deer excused herself and went off to rest for the evening event, the Wheel Dance.

Jo Beth accompanied Colter to the paddock to

get Chieftain. She stood by the fence listening as he patted the horse's muzzle and spoke in rapid and fluid Athabascan. She closed her eyes and let the music of his voice wash over her. At that moment she thought that she could live and die on that mountain as long she could hear Colter's magical, mystical voice.

She couldn't have said exactly when sparks had changed to love, but she suspected the transition had something to do with that wonderful voice. Hugging her arms around her waist, she let herself drift and dream under the spell of Colter speaking his Apache language.

"Napping, Jo Beth?"

Her eyes snapped open. Napping was as good an excuse as any, she decided. "How can I ever keep a secret if you keep sneaking up on me like that?"

"I never sneak. I walk without sound. It's the Apache way." He held out one hand. "Come."

She put her hand in his and followed him to the barn to ready Chieftain for the cross-country race. He threw the blanket across the stallion and walked him out into the sunshine. Then he mounted and leaned down to Jo Beth.

"Will you be waiting for me at the finish line?"

"Yes. Nothing could keep me away, Colter."

He leaned closer. "A kiss for luck before I go?"

She stood on tiptoe and kissed him. When the kiss ended, she stepped back. "I'll follow you to the starting point in the truck."

"You need your rest for the night ahead."

"Doctor's orders?"

He smiled. "Doctor's suggestion. I would never dare give you orders, Jo Beth McGill. I still remember that big stick."

"It's a darned good thing you do." She sprinted

off, calling as she ran. "See you at the starting point."

She whistled for Zar and climbed into the truck, and they headed back into the small village. She was there long before Colter, for he wanted to save Chieftain for the long ride ahead.

When she saw him coming, she separated herself from the crowd. He galloped toward her, so magnificent on his white stallion that he brought tears to her eyes.

"You belong here, Colter," she whispered to herself, "in a way that I never can."

Colter drew the stallion to a halt beside her and leaned far down to catch her face. "Wait for me, Jo Beth."

"I'll wait forever if I have to."

He pressed his lips against hers, and then he was gone. She watched him line up with the other men who would ride the grueling cross-country race. There were four of them, but the most magnificent of all was Colter.

The signal was given, and the riders were off. Hooves drummed upon the ground and dust spewed up behind them. She shaded her eyes, straining to keep Colter and Chieftain in her sight as long as she could. The men rode hard and expertly, leaning low over their mounts so that they seemed to be a part of the animals they rode. Finally Colter was nothing more than a speck of white in the distance. Only then did she turn and head back to his mother's ranch.

"I could borrow a nice Indian dress for you."

Little Deer sat in the rocking chair and watched the future mother of her grandchildren come out in a dress that looked like something those soap-opera women wore on television.

"That's kind of you, but I'm not a nice Indian. I'm a blond-haired, blue-eyed woman who has gone and fallen in love with a nice Indian."

Little Deer laughed. "You have spunk, don't you?"

"I always have and I always will." She lifted the skirt of her blue halter dress. "I hope it's not too showy."

"My son has the blood of chiefs in his veins. It is appropriate that his woman be the most richly dressed at the dance." She left her chair and touched the skirt of Jo Beth's dress. "It looks like summer clouds. What is that material called?"

"Chiffon."

"I had to know so I could brag to Bessie Running Water." She linked arms with Jo Beth. "We will go now."

Little Deer had slept late, so they were among the last to reach the village. Pleading old age, Little Deer elected to wait in the truck while Jo waited at the finish line.

Jo Beth merged into the crowd, pressing as close to the finish line as she could. All around her, people were talking about the cross-country race. Some were placing bets and some were telling stories, and everyone had a different story to tell.

"They say Big Elk was ahead at the bend of the river."

"One saw the white stallion. It's Gray Wolf, not Big Elk."

"No. Runners were sent into the mountains. The white stallion lost his footing. Gray Wolf is down."

Jo Beth thought she would faint. She turned to the last speaker, a big man she hadn't remembered seeing that morning.

"Has something happened to Colter?" She plucked his sleeve. "Please, I have to know."

"Runners carried a litter into the mountains. Some say his skull was crushed."

All the air left her lungs. "Where?" Her voice was barely a whisper.

"In the Bear Canyons."

Her mind raced. She had to get to Colter. What would be best for him? Should she wait for the runners to return so she could load him up quickly and take him to the nearest hospital, or should she ask someone to drive her into the canyons? Could she even get there in the truck?

"Someone's coming." The cry went up, and the entire crowd tensed. From a distance came the thundering of horse's hooves.

Jo Beth didn't wait at the finish line. She broke free of the crowd and ran toward the approaching rider. Every beat of the horse's hooves vibrated through her. Her high heels felt as if they would crack under the pressure and her lungs burned with the effort, but still she ran. When she was free of the crowd, free of the village, she stopped to catch her breath. Panting, she hung her head down.

It was then that she heard her name being called.

"Jo! JO!"

She jerked her head up, and there, coming down from the mountain, was Colter, bending low over the head of his white stallion. Relief made her so weak she almost sank to the ground.

She lifted one hand, and he raced toward her. The stallion, set on gaining the finish line, whinnied sharply and reared in the air when Colter brought him to a stop.

He gentled the horse with his hands until only a tremor betrayed his nervousness. Jo ran to him.

"Colter! You're safe."

"Jo, what's wrong?" Colter bent down to her and put one hand on her face. "You're pale."

"I thought you were hurt. Oh, Colter. I thought you were dead." Her hand trembled on his leg.

He slid off the horse and gathered her into his arms. With his hands on her bare back, he soothed her. "There, sweet. There, Yellow Bird." He pressed his lips into her hair. "Tell me what's wrong."

"Back at the village they said a man had been hurt."

"Where?"

"The Bear Canyons. Runners have been sent."

"They would take the narrow path, the short-cut. It's difficult on a horse, but not impossible." He made a swift decision. "My bag is in the truck. I'll leave you back at the village."

"I'm going with you, Colter." She kicked off her shoes. "I've done enough volunteer hospital work to be of help."

He nodded, then vaulted onto the horse. With one hand he drew Jo Beth up behind him.

"Hold on tight, Jo."

They raced toward the village.

Eight

It took them almost an hour to get to the fallen man.

The trail was steep and winding, and Colter couldn't hurry for fear of his horse losing footing. Halfway up the trail they came upon the runners. Colter stopped long enough to tell them that he would go ahead with his medical bag and that they should continue with the litter.

"How will we ever find him?" Jo asked.

"The course is well known to anyone who has ever ridden it. I know approximately where a rider could have gone over."

She shivered and squeezed her arms tighter around his waist. "I'm glad it wasn't you. I couldn't stand it if anything happened to you."

"Nothing will ever happen to me, Jo Beth. I'm indestructible."

"You're not."

"Doctors have to be."

He laughed, but there was no mirth in the sound. Colter Gray Wolf was far from being mirthful. Never had his betrayal of his people weighed more heavily on him. A thousand *if onlys* played through his mind. If only he'd finished his clinic. If only he'd stayed. But regret changed nothing. It was best not to think of anything now except finding the hapless rider.

He concentrated on the trail. "Keep your eyes open, Jo. We're almost there. Look for any sign of horse or rider."

Colter saw the first sign, a gray filly, missing both blanket and rider.

"Clyde Lightfoot. At least the filly is unhurt. That's a good sign."

"Do you think he's close?"

"Yes. He's a good trainer. His filly would be trained to stay close."

Colter drew to a halt and dismounted. Then he helped Jo down. He smiled when he saw her stockinged feet.

"You'e liable to pick up a stone bruise with those bare feet."

"It's a small price to pay for knowing you're safe."

They followed the rim of the canyon for a few hundred feet, and then they saw Clyde. He was caught in a small crevice down the side of the canyon wall, and his head was bleeding profusely.

Colter leaned over the wall. "Clyde. Can you hear me?"

"Gray Wolf. Is that you?"

Clyde's voice was weak, but at least he was conscious. Colter was encouraged.

"I'm going to see if I can reach you. Hang on."

Colter stretched flat on the rocks and leaned far down over the wall. Loose rocks skittered over the rim and bounced down to the bottom of the canyon.

"Be careful, Colter."

"I can't reach you, Clyde. Hold on a while longer."

Colter raised himself up and whistled for his

horse. Chieftain trotted to his side. Colter stroked his muzzle and talked to him in Athabascan. Then he began to unfasten the halter.

"What are you doing?"

"Using this halter as an extension to lower myself over the wall." Jo Beth paled. "Fate was smiling on Clyde today. Six years ago we didn't use these leather halters for the races."

He lashed one end of the leather halter around his right leg and tied the other around the leg of his stallion. "Don't make a move, Jo. Don't make a sound."

"Will he stand for you?"

"If he remembers his training he will."

She held her breath while Colter maneuvered himself over the wall. A thousand horrors came to her mind—the horse bolting, dragging Colter across the rocks; the leather breaking, plunging Colter into the canyon floor; the horse rearing up in fright, stomping Colter to pieces.

None of that happened. Colter gave a few short commands, and Chieftain began to back slowly. Colter reappeared over the wall, pulling Clyde with him.

In short order Colter had untied himself and was treating Clyde's injuries. Jo squatted beside him, handing him gauze pads.

"It's not as bad as it looks. There are some bleeders on the scalp that always make head injuries look fatal. It's just a small gash." Colter's fingers were nimble as he talked. "The biggest injury is this broken finger."

Clyde's middle finger was twisted, so that it pointed backward. Colter gave him a shot for pain, them quickly set and splinted the finger.

By the time he was finished, the runners had arrived. Colter helped them put Clyde on the litter, then promised to visit him early the next morning. He stood, watching them disappear.

He had that quiet, faraway look on his face that Jo had come to dread. Cold fingers of premonition dragged up her spine.

"Colter."

He turned to her. "We'll stay a while so that Chieftain can rest. He's been ridden hard today." He took the blanket off the horse and spread it on the rocks. "It will be sweaty, but it's the best I can offer right now."

Colter sat down and leaned against a rock. Jo sat beside him, hugging her knees. He made no move to reach for her. She felt a chill wind bite at her bare back, but she didn't shiver. Right now she wanted Colter's confidence, not his sympathy, and she sensed that he was ready to give it.

"I'm glad you came with me, Jo. You made a good nurse. Thanks."

"Anytime, Doctor."

She laid her head on her knees and studied him. He was gazing down the trail, the way they had come.

"What do you see, Colter?"

"The past." She waited, never taking her eyes from his face. "When I was young I dreamed of being a doctor. My parents dreamed of it too. But my dream was different from theirs. I pictured myself in a large hospital in a large city—in the white man's world, Jo—and they pictured me in the village, helping my people."

"You achieved your dream."

"At what cost?" He got up and walked away.

She saw the tenseness in his stance, the tight muscles in his back. Her first impulse was to go to him, to put her arms around him and comfort him, but every instinct told her to stay. Over and over Colter had told her that he had to make his journey of the soul alone. And now he was making it. The only difference was that he was letting her share the journey. She wouldn't betray that trust.

She sat very still on the blanket, waiting for him to speak, letting him decide what he would tell her and letting him tell it in his own way.

"I was born Apache, grew up Apache, but something inside me longed for more. If there were cultural and social boundaries, I was determined to cross them. And I did. But in the process, I lost my identity."

He walked along the rim of the canyon, challenging Fate. Twice his feet loosened rocks and sent them spinning to the canyon floor. Jo Beth put her hands over her mouth to keep from crying out. When he was almost too far away for her to see, he picked up a rock and flung it into space. From somewhere far below, a raven sounded its call.

Colter listened to the plaintive cry of the raven. Its lonesome sound was a foreboding. He knew what he must do. He guessed he'd known all along, but it had taken Clyde's accident to give him the push he needed.

He turned and looked back at Jo Beth, sitting on the blanket, her head resting quietly on her knees. *She knows,* he thought. Sorrow tore at him and a lonesome, primitive cry of despair ripped straight up from his heart. He bit back the cry so that it was no more than a moaning that blended with the winds in the canyon.

It is time, he said to himself. He went back to Jo and stood on the edge of the blanket, looking down at her.

"Are you cold, Jo?"

"No." It was a lie. She was not cold on the outside, but inside she was a glacier.

He began his story without preliminaries, hoping that the quickness would lessen the pain.

"San Francisco cast its spell and wooed me away from my people. I came to visit. I was a good son in that respect. And four years ago, I even started building a clinic."

"The one I saw?"

"Yes. I was on summer vacation here, and it seemed the right thing to do. My parents were pleased and honored. I left at the end of the summer, thinking I would finish the clinic on my next vacation. But when I came back it was too late." He sat on the blanket, his legs crossed, his hands propped on his knees, staring at the darkening sky. "It was the following summer, three years ago. I got the call in the middle of the night. My father was sick." He turned to look at her, and the raw emotion on his face made her cry out. "It was pancreatitis, Jo. And by the time I got here it was too late."

"I'm so sorry, Colter."

"While he lay dying, he called for me. I will never forget how his hand felt, dry and already turning cold. He said to me, 'Promise me . . . promise me that you will come home, Gray Wolf.' I made that promise, Jo. It was a promise I never kept."

She came to him then. All his barriers were down, and she could comfort him. Circling one arm around him, she cradled his head against her shoulder.

"I betrayed him and I betrayed my people."

"How can you say that?"

"If I had finished the clinic, my father might have lived. There was no hospital nearby, no good doctor. I let my father die."

She stroked his hair. "Who do you think you are, Colter Gray Wolf? No man has the power over life and death."

"When you're a doctor, Jo, you sometimes believe you do."

She bent down and kissed the top of his head. "Thank you for confiding in me, Colter."

Instead of answering, he straightened up and took her in his arms. With her head tucked under his chin, he hugged her close to his chest. They stayed that way a long while.

And then his hand began to caress her bare back. The strokes were slow and lazy at first. Gradually they became more sensuous. Shivers crawled along her skin.

She lifted her face to look at him. His eyes had become hooded.

"Jo," he whispered.

She put her arms around his neck and their lips came together. All the pain he had bottled up for so long came pouring out, metamorphosed as passion. With his lips on hers, he unhooked her halter and pushed the soft chiffon aside. His hands cradled her back as he kissed her shoulders.

"Colter." She tangled her hands in his hair, pulling him closer. "Ahh, Colter."

He lowered her to the blanket and undressed her with great and tender care. The sky was so close, she could almost reach out and touch it. In its velvety dark reaches, one single star shone. She gazed straight at the star and wished the night would never end.

Colter hovered above her, memorizing her with his hands and chanting the ancient love songs of the Apache. He came to her, and it was like the first time, with its wonder and exquisite beauty.

They soared together, time and time again. And

Jo Beth knew he was saying good-bye. He never spoke her name. He didn't call her Yellow Bird. He didn't call her his woman. He spoke only two languages—the language of his people and the language of love.

And when it was over, he held her close. She pressed her face into the curve between his cheek and his shoulder.

"That was good-bye, wasn't it, Colter?"

"Yes."

"Why?"

"I'm a betrayer, Jo. I can't ask you to share my life until it's straightened out. I must atone for my sins."

She never knew that love could hurt so much. The fear that had been building in her since she came to his mountain bubbled to the surface, and on its heel came anger, anger at Fate, anger at the past, anger at the Apache, and most of all, anger at him.

She raised herself on her elbow and looked at him. "And you want me to go home like an obedient woman and wait for you to decide when you're good enough for me?"

"I wouldn't put it like that, Jo."

"Then how would you put it?"

He caught her shoulder. "You're angry. It's bad to make decisions while you're angry."

"You've already made the decision, Colter." She reached for her dress. "You're as stubborn as this rock." She slapped her hand down on the blanket. "Nothing I can say or do at this point will change your mind."

"You know me too well."

He put on his jeans and reached to fasten her dress, but she stepped back.

"I might as well get used to doing this by myself."

"Jo, I don't want you to go like this."

"How do you want me to go, Colter? Laughing? Pretending that there's a Santa Claus and that he's going to come down my chimney next Christmas, bringing a ready and willing Apache doctor?"

"Don't, Jo." He took her into his arms, stroking her stiff body until she yielded.

She clung to him. "I hate you for this, Colter." Her voice was muffled against his chest.

"No you don't. You're hurting right now. I'm so sorry it had to be this way." He pressed his face into her hair. "If it's any consolation, I'm hurting too, Jo."

She was silent a long time, filled with remorse. "Let me stay. Let me help you."

"I have to do this alone."

He swayed, rocking her in his arms, cradling her next to his heart. They stayed that way for a long time, and then he spoke.

"I want you to wait for me, Jo."

"Colter, you've called me your woman and I've followed you. You've held out your hand and I've come to you." She leaned away so she could look at his face. "I don't know what I'll do. I'm not a patient Apache. I'm just a Mississippi girl trying to endure the best way I know how."

"Don't underestimate yourself. You not only endure, you triumph." He whistled for his horse, then leaned down and kissed her tenderly on the lips. It was time to let her go. Fate had brought her and Fate was taking her away. "Be safe, Jo. Be happy."

She wondered how she expected her to be happy with a broken heart, but she didn't say anything.

"You, too, Colter."

He picked up the blanket, slung it on the stallion, and mounted. Jo didn't wait for him to hold out his hand. That small, familiar gesture would have been enough to send her over the edge. She was already too close to a crying jag for her comfort.

She reached up for him, and he pulled her onto the stallion. Together they rode off into the darkness, taking the long and safe way home.

She held on to him on their long ride back, but it was almost as if she were touching a stranger. Colter had already separated himself from her mentally. For all the communication there was between them, she might as well have been in Mississippi.

It was late by the time they reached his home. Colter rode straight into the barn and silently dismounted. He held his arms up to Jo Beth, and she automatically slid into them.

For a moment he held her close. She pressed her cheek against his chest so she could hear the steady thumping of his heart.

"My heart is naked, Jo," he whispered. "It bleeds."

"Mine too."

She lifted her head and looked into his face. "There is another way, Colter."

"No. One life in limbo is enough."

She thought briefly about arguing, but she knew that in the end it would be useless. If she'd learned one thing about Colter, it was his determination to behave nobly. Instead of arguing, she traced the lines of his face with her fingers.

"The camera can't capture this," she said. "The texture of your skin, the proud bone structure, the fine glow, as if God had hidden a sunset just underneath your skin."

"Jo . . ." He caught her hand and kissed the palm. He was tempted to change his mind. Almost, he asked her to stay. His eyes darkened with pain as he released her and stepped back. "I'll see to Chieftain."

"Yes. He's had a hard day."

She left the barn quickly so Colter wouldn't see the tears. They filled her eyes and spilled down her cheeks.

"I won't cry," she said.

Her dog came up and pushed against her legs, rubbing his big head on her calves in joyful greeting. She knelt beside him. Colter's brother and his wife had taken care of Zar and Little Deer, driving them home after the accident in the canyon.

"I'm glad to see you too, boy." The red-gold tail thumped the ground. "You might as well pack your bags, Zar. We're going home."

She wiped her face with the back of her hand, went into the house, and found Little Deer waiting for them in the den. Suddenly it occurred to her that she had more than one good-bye to say.

Little Deer sat in the rocking chair, her hands folded and her face serene. "The trip was successful."

Jo sat facing her on the sofa. "Yes."

Little Deer nodded. "Gray Wolf always succeeds. He is destined for greatness."

"I believe so."

The clock on the wall marked time while Little Deer rocked and Jo Beth pondered. At last she decided there was no easy way to say good-bye.

"I'll be leaving tomorrow, Little Deer."

"My child, yesterday that would have made me happy."

Jo Beth smiled. "Thank you, Little Deer."

"Will you come back?"

"I don't know."

Little Deer stared into space a long time before

she spoke. "You will come back. Gray Wolf has chosen you. He will not let you go."

Jo Beth started to say that he already had, but she decided that would be a betrayal.

"I'll send you the pictures, Little Deer. I'll call from time to time to find out how you are."

"Your heart is good, Jo Beth. My son has chosen wisely."

Jo Beth couldn't say more for the lump in her throat. Instead, she went to the old woman and kissed her cheek. Then she quickly left the room.

Colter stayed in the barn longer than necessary. There was a heaviness in him that was more than fatigue. It was the heaviness of despair. When Jo Beth had walked out of the barn, he had felt all the poetry and music of his soul go with her.

He sat on a bale of hay and tried to analyze the situation objectively. But love made objectivity impossible. That was the only consolation he had at the moment: He had never told her he loved her. He had never made promises to her that he couldn't keep.

The house was dark when he finally left the barn and went inside. It was just as well. He felt drained of all feeling, drained of life.

He made his way to his wing of the house and prepared for bed. The sheets looked inviting after the trying day, and he lay upon them naked. From deep within the sleeping house came the sounds of night—a muted groaning as the old wooden floors settled down to rest, a soft scurrying as the house mouse came out looking for crumbs, a muted tapping as the north wind rose and banged the shutters against the outside walls.

The darkness brought more than night noises:

It brought need so sharp he cried out. He rose from his bed and walked to the window. Jo Beth and the night went together. He had become addicted to her. As he looked out at the blackness, he knew she was an addiction he would never be rid of. Nor did he want to be rid of her. He would hold her next to his heart always.

He stood at the window, gazing into the endless night.

Jo Beth woke up when the first rays of light came through her window. During the night she had decided that partings were best done quickly. She had also decided to go out with style. It was the McGill way. Tears and groaning didn't lessen the pain.

She dressed and began to pack her bags, being careful not to make noises and wake Little Deer. The packing didn't take long. She was holding the last item, the blue chiffon dress, when Colter spoke.

"I will always remember that dress."

She turned slowly, still holding the blue dress. He was leaning against the door frame watching her, his arms folded across his broad chest.

"How long have you been there, Colter?"

"Long enough to question my judgment a hundred times."

She gave him a gay smile. "You were right. This never would have worked." She folded the dress quickly and stuffed it into her suitcase. Then she snapped the lid so the dress would be out of sight. She didn't want any reminders of that good-bye on the mountain. Turning from the suitcase, she smiled at him again. "I don't know why I ever believed I could be your woman, Colter. I simply don't have time. Anyway, I still don't believe in love."

"Don't, Jo."

"Don't what?"

"Don't deny what we had."

"What did we have?"

"Something beautiful."

She almost lost her nerve. Almost, but not quite. "It was great while it lasted. You're a superb lover. I'm going to mark that interlude in the desert as one of the best times I've ever had."

She reached for her suitcase, but he was already across the room. Their hands met as he took the case from her. In that brief moment, time and place ceased to exist. There were only the two of them and a love so bright and shining it couldn't be denied.

She was the first to pull away. "I have no regrets, Colter. But I do have a million obligations, and so do you." She held out her hand. "Friends?"

He took it. "Always, Jo." He started for the door with her suitcase. There was nothing else to say. He knew the time had come to let her go. "I'll drive you into Phoenix."

"I'd rather do this alone, Colter. Airports are too sterile for good-byes. I want to remember you in the mountains with the wind in your hair and the sun at your back."

Together they walked to the rented truck. Colter loaded her bags and helped her get Zar settled onto the front seat. When she got behind the wheel, he leaned into the open window and cupped her face. His thumbs circled her jaw and he looked deep into her eyes, as if he were trying to absorb her spirit.

"Good-bye, Yellow Bird."

She couldn't speak. It was the first time he'd

called her Yellow Bird since the mountain accident. And she knew it would be the last. She lifted her hand in salute, and put the truck in gear.

He stepped back and watched her leave his mountain, straining his eyes until the truck was a puff of dust in the distance. Letting her go was one of the hardest things he'd ever done.

Jo Beth battled tears on the drive to Phoenix, and once she'd reached the city, having to tend to business matters kept her sane. She returned the rental truck, saw that Zar was properly prepared for the flight, then boarded the plane for home.

Back in Tupelo she crammed so many insignificant and unnecessary details into each day that she didn't have time to think, didn't have time to hurt. She lived each day for itself, not looking forward and never, never looking back.

"Jo, if I light all these candles, I'm liable to set the house on fire. How old are you anyway?"

"Light the candles, Andrew, and hush."

October had brought many things to Mississippi—painted leaves, balmy weather, and another birthday for Jo Beth. The whole family had gathered at her parents' house for the celebration. The rest of the clan were gathered in the backyard, watching Rick's three boys fight over whose turn it was on the tire swing, while she and Andrew were in the kitchen getting the cake ready.

Andrew struck a match, then glanced at his sister and blew it out.

"Three weeks is a long time to mourn, Jo."

"Who's mourning?" She set the dessert plates on the table, then went to get the forks.

"You are. Have been ever since you got back from Arizona. What happened out there?"

"I don't want to talk about it." The forks rattled in the drawer.

If there was one thing Andrew McGill knew, it was when to shut up and when to keep talking. The time had come to keep talking.

He struck the match and held it to one of the pink candles. When the flame caught, he lit the second while the match was still burning far enough away from the stem not to singe his fingers. With the two candles glowing, he threw the burned match away and started toward his sister.

He put one hand on her shoulder, and she jumped as if she'd been bitten. She whirled around, holding on to three forks.

"What in the world? Andrew, you haven't finished lighting the candles."

"The candles can wait."

"The next thing you know, Rick's three boys will be in here howling for cake."

"Let the little rascals howl. It would serve Rick right for fathering three little rogues just like himself."

"I won't tell him you said that." She punched him playfully on the shoulder. "Go finish with the cake."

"Not until I know why you came back from Arizona looking like a wet chicken with all its tail feathers plucked."

"It's over and done with. Forget about it."

Andrew took her hand and led her to a kitchen chair. He hooked the chair with one foot, dragged it out, and gently pushed his sister onto the seat. Propping one foot on the chair's bottom rung, he grinned down at her.

"Jo, do you remember the time I got into that little trouble at school?"

"Andrew, setting the library on fire is not a *little* trouble."

"Okay. So it was *big* trouble, but it was an accident." He grinned. "The point is, you were the one who told me that if I didn't confess, it would turn me black inside, and a little bit of me would die."

"I didn't say that . . . *turn you black inside.* Gracious, Andrew, you make me sound like some kind of nut."

"We were only eight and ten at the time. I've always thought it was rather precocious of you." He cupped her face. "What's turning you black inside, Jo?"

Jo felt the tears she'd held back for three weeks pushing against her eyelids. It had been three weeks since she'd left Colter, she thought, and she hadn't cried. Not once.

One tear trickled down her cheek, and then another and another, until the floodgates were open. Andrew squatted beside her, and she leaned on him and cried. Jo Beth had never cried in a ladylike manner. She whooped and wailed and bawled. Her eyes puffed up and her nose turned red. But when the jag was over, she felt cleansed.

She finally raised her head and looked at her brother. "I messed up your shirt."

"Feel better?"

"Yes."

"Want to talk now?"

"I didn't believe there was such a thing as falling in love until I met Colter Gray Wolf. Dad had captured him and tied him in the outhouse."

Andrew laughed. "When I get ready to settle down with a woman, maybe Dad will do the same thing for me."

She wiped her face with the back of her hand

and sniffed. Then she smiled. "For the first time in my life I felt honest-to-goodness sparks."

"Then why aren't you out there in Arizona instead of here in Tupelo blowing out thirty-one birthday candles?"

"Twenty-nine."

"Again?"

"Twenty-nine is a nice age. I'm going to stay that way a few more years." Her face grew serious again. "Colter loves me, Andrew. I know he does. But there are some problems in his life that he wants to resolve on his own."

"How long will that take?"

"He didn't say."

"And you're just going to wait around here and find out? That's not like a McGill."

Andrew was goading her. She could tell by that devilish twinkle in his eyes. Suddenly she knew that a good challenge was exactly what she needed. She'd never been one to sit around and wait for something to happen. In the McGill tradition, she'd always gone out and *made* something happen.

She stood up and pushed aside her chair. "Can you and Rick come by and check on Mom and Dad every few days?"

"Are you going somewhere, Jo?" His grin was as lazy and charming as his drawl.

"I'm going courting, Mississippi style." She picked up the matchbox and began to light her birthday candles. "Remember this, little brother: Life without love is just a succession of birthdays." With the candles lit, she picked up the cake. "Let's take this out to Rick's darling little savages."

"I won't tell him you said that. He thinks they're perfect."

Jo Beth and Andrew stepped out the door with

the cake and were immediately attacked by three little boys, laughing and yelling for cake. Rick McGill sat in the glider with his arm around his very pregnant wife and smiled indulgently.

"Careful with your auntie, boys. She's getting too old for that rough-and-tumble stuff."

Martha Ann punched her husband playfully in the ribs. "Behave yourself, Rick McGill."

"Have I ever, sweetheart?"

She patted her oversize stomach and smiled. "No, and I hope you never do."

Andrew rolled his eyes heavenward. "Love. It's enough to give a fellow a bellyache. Jo, are you sure you want to end up like those two?" He nodded toward his brother and sister-in-law.

"Positive." Grinning, she put the cake on the picnic table and patted her flat stomach. "Except maybe not that part."

Martha Ann rose from her seat on the glider and waddled majestically across the backyard, her stomach preceding her. "You'll change your mind, Jo Beth. And I'll be there to say *I told you so.*" She caught Michael's hand right before he plunged it into the top of the cake.

Rick followed his wife and picked up Matthew, who was intent on feeding Zar two birthday candles. "What's this about love, Jo? Who is this man and will I approve?"

Jo got a gleam in her eye. "You still keep in touch with the Donovan family, don't you, Rick?" Without waiting for a reply, she plucked little Matthew out of his arms and deposited him on Sara McGill's lap. Sara began to coo over her grandson, while Silas, who had been dreaming about the time he'd been a cowpuncher down in Texas, looked at the little boy and wondered why nobody had told him he had a new son.

Jo Beth linked her arm through Rick's and led him back to the glider.

"Come on, big brother, you and I have work to do."

"What kind of work?"

"We're going to lay battle plans."

Colter sat on the deck of his houseboat and looked out across the bay. It felt good to be back. He propped his feet on the railing, leaned back in his deck chair, and closed his eyes. He was tired. It had been three weeks, four days, and seven hours since he'd last seen Jo Beth. And he'd filled every minute to cover the pain.

He had to stop thinking about her. There was too much to do. The clinic in the White Mountains was being rebuilt, and every day there was another problem that he had to handle via the telephone. Then there was his practice. It seemed that everyone in San Francisco had waited until he came back to have a gall bladder attack. In addition, there was the problem of what to do once the clinic was finished. Would he go back and set up practice there? Could he ever be content with a small general practice after years of challenging work in a big hospital? On the other hand, could he live with himself if he didn't go back?

One thing he'd discovered in his lonely desert vigil: he was Apache, not just by birth but in spirit. And that would never change.

The jangling of the telephone interrupted his thoughts. For a second he thought about not answering it. One of the things he'd loved most about being in the desert was not having a telephone to disturb the peace. It jangled again, and he got up to answer it. In his profession the phone was a necessary inconvenience.

"Colter. What's up, buddy?"

It was Jim Roman, sounding as cheerful and perky as an eighteen-year-old going out on a Saturday night date.

"I'm not on call tonight, if that's what you're asking."

"Good. I have two tickets to the National League playoffs. Just the thing to cure your blues."

"Who said I have the blues?"

"For once in your life, your face gives you away. Since you've come back from that desert you've been lower than a toad in a hailstorm."

Colter laughed. "All right. I have the blues and I'm missing Jo Beth like hell and if a baseball game is the cure, I'm willing to go."

"Good. I'll pick you up in thirty minutes. And Colter, take off those damned moccasins and put on jogging shoes like the rest of us ordinary people. I don't want you upstaging me."

"How did you know I was wearing moccasins?"

"I knew. See you later."

Colter hung up the phone, changed into jogging shoes, and started to go topside. On second thought, he grabbed his baseball cap and rammed it on his head, then climbed the ladder to wait for Jim.

When she saw him appear on deck wearing his baseball cap, Jo Beth laughed with wicked glee. She'd been peeping out the porthole of Jim Roman's houseboat for the last hour, watching Colter. She'd been in San Francisco only three hours, and already her plan was set in motion. When it was all over she'd have to thank Jim and Hannah

Donovan Roman properly. She'd invite them to the wedding.

She let the curtain fall back over the porthole and sat on the bunk, hugging her knees. She'd give Jim and Colter time to get to Candlestick Park. There was no hurry. She knew her seat was directly in front of Colter's. Jim had seen to that.

She left her bunk and began to dress. She put on the snuggest jeans she had, then topped them off with a blue sweater that made her eyes look like a little bit of heaven and her hair look like fairies' wings, even if she did say so herself. Phase One of her plan was "Playing Hard to Get," and she was dressed to thrill.

It was only the bottom of the second, and San Francisco was already two runs ahead. Colter clutched his hot dog in one hand and his beer in the other and leaned forward for a better view.

There was a small commotion at the end of the bleachers, and he glanced that way to see what was happening. A blond woman was inching her way through the crowded seats, and, just his luck, she was headed his way. She'd probably end up right in front of him, and more than likely she'd be the kind who would leave every few minutes to go to the bathroom and powder her nose.

He started to turn back to the ball game, and then he did a double take. The woman looked like Jo Beth. Disgusted with himself, he turned his attention to the batter. That wasn't the first time he'd been startled. Nearly every slender, blond-haired woman he'd seen lately had reminded him of Jo Beth.

Colter settled back to watch the game. The count was ball three, strike two, and the hitter was San

Francisco's secret weapon, a rookie the team had called up from the minor leagues. The pitcher was poised, the batter was ready . . . and Colter squeezed his hot dog in two. Ketchup ran down his fingers, and a glob of mustard plopped onto the knee of his pants. His pulse accelerated and his blood pressure rose.

The crowd was on its feet, yelling and screaming, but he had no idea what it was all about. Jo Beth McGill had taken the seat directly in front of him. Apparently she hadn't seen him, for she'd never even looked his way.

She settled into her seat and her back brushed against his legs. A strand of her glorious hair fanned out and rested on his blue jeans. He stared at it as if he had never seen hair.

"Wasn't that great, buddy?" Jim pounded him on the shoulder.

"Yes." Candlestick Park could have been on fire, and he would never have known. He sat, mesmerized by a single strand of golden hair.

"What's the matter, Colter? You look like you're having a heart attack."

"Indigestion." Colter wiped the mustard off his jeans and pressed the half-eaten hot dog into the napkins. His hunger was no longer for hot dogs.

"Take an antacid tablet," Jim laughed as he turned back to the game.

Colter stood up. The action was reflexive. He had to move, to go somewhere, to do something, to do *anything* except sit and stare at Jo Beth's hair.

Jim glanced up at him, still grinning. "Going somewhere?"

"I have to . . . throw away this hot dog." He didn't exit; he retreated. Geronimo would have disowned him.

Jo Beth heard him leave. She gave him time to be out of sight, then turned around and grinned.

"My little plan seems to be working," she said. Then she sobered. "Do you think I'm being too hard on him?"

Jim Roman laughed heartily. "My dear Jo Beth, a man like Colter needs to suffer before he gets his woman. Believe me, I know. You should have seen what Hannah Donovan put me through."

"I can't thank the two of you enough for helping me."

"We would have been disappointed not to be in on this scheme. Anyhow, we're glad to have somebody using the houseboat, and it's good that Hannah has her mind on something else these last few days before the baby comes."

"Tell me, Jim. How is he . . . really? When I called his mother and found out he'd come back here, I didn't know what to think."

"He's stoic, as always, but . . . shhh, here he comes."

Jo Beth quickly faced the field and became absorbed in the game. She was only pretending, though. She heard the rustlings as Colter took his seat directly behind her. The hairs stood up on her arms. He had to have recognized her by now. When would he acknowledge her? What would he say? Would he be polite? Distant? Cordial? Cold? And what would she say? She hadn't thought that far ahead. She'd never played hard to get. She'd never played any lover's game. Rick, who was an old hand at games, had given her some pointers, and Andrew, who thought he knew something about everything, had tried to tell her exactly what to do, but she'd finally given up trying to learn from them. She told them she'd wing it.

A trickle of sweat inched down her back as she

tried to act nonchalant. She was dying to get another look at Colter. The batter gave her a chance. He hit a high pop foul outside left field, and she turned halfway around to watch the ball. One more slight turn, and she was face-to-face with Colter.

"Colter!"

"Jo Beth!"

They both pretended surprise. She held out her hand, and he gave it a polite shake.

"What an unexpected pleasure," she said.

"What brings you to San Francisco, Jo Beth?"

You, she wanted to say. But that wouldn't do. "Business." She gave him a wicked smile of satisfaction. "You can let go of my hand now."

He circled his forefinger on the underside of her wrist before he released her. She almost abandoned her game and threw herself into his arms, right there in Candlestick Park. Instead she put her hand primly in her lap.

"Another assignment?" he asked.

"Yes." She didn't elaborate. "You've cut your hair."

"Yes. The braids didn't make me Indian."

"No, they made you sexy."

The minute the words were out she could have bitten off her tongue. If Colter had laughed, she probably would have. Fortunately for her, he didn't.

"You thought so, did you?"

I still do, she wanted to say. But she didn't. Instead she looked out over the baseball field, feigning a great interest.

"We're missing the game," she said.

"On the contrary. I think this is the best game in town." He smiled, then, for the first time since she'd come into the ballpark.

He was on to her, she thought. Why had she

ever thought she could fool Colter Gray Wolf? There was nothing to do but go on pretending. She'd come all the way from Mississippi to chase this man until he caught her, and she wasn't about to back down now.

She stared boldly at him, trying to think of a suitably flip reply. That's when she saw the stain on his pants. Colter Gray Wolf had invented neat. Even after he'd raced cross-country and rescued Clyde from the canyon, he'd still somehow managed to look unmussed. She grinned.

"You have mustard on your pants, Colter."

"They don't make hot dogs like they used to. One bite and they fall apart."

"You'll have to be more careful."

He gave her a long look then, one that sizzled every hair on her head.

"So I will."

She turned back to watch the game so fast, she made jackrabbits look slow. *Derned his hide, as Dad would say.* She never should have let him out of the privy. Then none of this would have happened.

Nine

Colter stared at the back of Jo Beth's head for five minutes, trying to figure out what was going on. While he mused, Jim gave a running commentary of the game.

"What a play! Did you see the way that ball curved?"

"Umm-hmm." All Colter saw was the way the lights made Jo's hair shine.

"What's he doing, using a relief pitcher?"

What was she doing in San Francisco?

"There goes the manager to the mound."

There she goes, turning her head so I can see her profile. Does she know I'm looking?

"I believe he's up to something."

I believe she's up to something.

Jo Beth shifted in her seat, and Colter had to adjust his own seating in order to keep his view of her profile. She was more beautiful than he remembered. Her skin was silkier. He had to clench his hands at his sides to keep from reaching out to touch her. He'd forfeited that right on the mountaintop. At least for a while. He couldn't change his mind now. He couldn't lean over and say, "Jo Beth, since you're here, why don't you come back to the houseboat with me?" He couldn't use her to satisfy his own selfish needs, then tell her that he still couldn't make any commitments because his own future was in limbo. The best thing for both of them would be for him to keep his distance.

Jo Beth must have felt him staring at her, because she turned and winked. Keeping his distance was forgotten. He leaned toward her.

"Jo Beth, are you flirting with me?"

"Would I flirt with you, Colter Gray Wolf?"

"I don't know. Would you?"

She pretended to think about his question for a while. It gave her a golden opportunity to feast her eyes on him. He made her throat go dry. He made her mouth water. And he set off so many sparks, she thought her sweater might catch on fire.

If she had ever had doubts about what she was doing, they all vanished. Colter had said he had to make his journey of the soul alone, but he'd been wrong. Instinctively she knew that. It was right for people in love to share. Not just joy, but pain as well. And while she would never try to influence his decision, there was no reason she had to stay in Mississippi while he made it.

"It all depends on what I would gain." She smiled at him. "What would I gain if I flirted with you, Colter?"

"Perhaps more than you bargained for."

He reached out and touched her cheek. The brief contact startled them both. He had meant to remain staunch, and she had meant to remain cool. Neither of them succeeded. When he pulled back, her face was warm and his pulse was running away.

"Careful what claims you make, Colter. I might challenge you."

He chuckled. "I'm glad you warned me, Jo Beth. I'll be on my guard."

"You do that." She winked again. "Enjoy the game," she said. Then she turned back around.

He stared at her back. *I wonder if I should ask where she's staying?*

She stared straight ahead. *I wonder if I should ask him to dinner?*

He watched the stadium lights play in her hair. *What would she do if I kissed her?*

She watched the peanut vendor selling his roasted nuts. *What would he do if I kissed him?*

He leaned to the left so he could see the side of her face. *Does she remember the sound of the turtledove?*

She slowly turned to see if she could catch a glimpse of him when he wasn't looking. *Does he remember the night he first covered me with his blanket?*

Suddenly she found herself staring into Colter's face.

"Jo Beth, I . . ."

"Colter, I . . ."

Both of them spoke at once.

"You first," he said.

"I thought I'd tell you good-bye, Colter."

"You're leaving?"

"Just the ballpark."

"Then you'll be here, in San Francisco?"

"For a while."

They gazed at each other. He wished that Fate hadn't decreed such a lonesome journey for him, and she wished she hadn't decided to play hard to get.

"Well . . ." She held out her hand. "Good-bye . . . again."

He squeezed her hand. Instead of letting it go, he lifted it to his lips. His breath warmed her palm and his mouth sent goose bumps skittering over her arms.

"Good-bye, Jo Beth. Take care."

She left the ballpark quickly. Never mind that the game wasn't over. Two things were of utmost importance: getting away from Colter before she ruined her carefully laid plans, and getting back to the houseboat before he did. He couldn't know that she was staying next door to him. At least, he couldn't know until the next day.

Colter watched her leave. Even after she had disappeared into the crowd, he still stared after her.

"Great game, isn't it, buddy?" Jim punched his shoulder.

"Yes. Great." Colter didn't even turn around. He continued staring into the distance, musing.

"Something interesting happening over there?" Jim suppressed his grin.

"No. Just watching the crowd."

"I see." This time, Jim couldn't keep from chuckling.

Colter shifted his attention back to the ball field. "Did I miss something funny?"

"No. I was just wondering what kind of excuse you'd think up if I called in your promise tomorrow."

"What promise?"

"To polish the brass on my boat. Remember? Back in Arizona."

"Yes. I remember. And certainly I'll do it. I'm off duty this weekend."

"Great. By the way, who was that gorgeous woman sitting in front of us?"

"Which woman?"

Jim had to squelch his laughter again. Colter might be an inscrutable Indian, but he was a terrible actor. "That blonde."

"That was Jo Beth McGill."

"The one you told me about? Well, hell, buddy, why didn't you introduce us?"

"She's no longer in my life."

Jim didn't say anything. He turned back to watch the game, grinning.

It was late by the time Colter got back to his houseboat. He should have been exhausted, but he wasn't. And he knew why. Jo Beth McGill.

He stood on his deck, leaning on the railing and looking out over the water. He had the eerie sensation that she was still close to him, so close he could reach out and touch her. He lifted his face to the stars to rid himself of the sensation. But it didn't help. Jo Beth was still with him, in his heart, in his mind, in his soul.

He hadn't counted on seeing her—at least, not so soon. But seeing her had made him question his judgment in sending her away. It was too late now, of course. He couldn't change the past.

He left the railing and went below deck to sleep.

Colter was accustomed to working long hours and sleeping very little. Even on the weekends when he was not on call, he kept his same habits.

On Sunday morning he got up with the sun, dressed in a pair of his oldest jeans, and made himself breakfast. Then he gathered his brass-polishing supplies and headed toward Jim Roman's boat.

It rocked and swayed when he climbed aboard. He stood a moment on the deck, refamiliarizing himself with the boat. He hadn't been on it in a long time. Since Jim and Hannah didn't live there anymore, it was seldom used. The last occasion had been a party on the bay for one of their children. And that had been back in May.

He stood a while longer, taking his bearing, then put down his supplies and began to polish the brass railing. He loved working with his hands. As the brass began to respond to his care, he started to whistle.

Below deck, Jo Beth sat straight up in her bed. Good grief, she thought. What time was it? She looked at her clock through sleep-squinty eyes. She couldn't believe what she was seeing. She never woke up at that goshawful time of day.

She'd started to lay her head back on the pillow when she heard the noise. Clutching the sheets around her neck, she listened. It wasn't a noise, it was whistling. Colter! It had to be Colter. Or else a happy burglar. Good grief.

She'd known he was coming; that was part of the plan. But she'd had no idea he would come this early. She'd planned to be up and dressed in full battle gear. She was going to be so polished and poised and desirable, he'd have to jump ship to cool himself off after looking at her.

Now she figured he'd jump ship anyway—in fright. She lay back against the pillows and groaned. In all her careful planning, she'd forgotten to tell Jim what time to send Colter over.

But all was not lost. He was on deck and she below. Maybe she could still get ruinously gorgeous before he saw her.

She eased one foot over the side of her bed, clutching the sheet around her. The whistling was louder now. He'd never whistled in the desert. She didn't even know he could.

She took a step and the boards under her feet creaked loudly enough to wake the dead.

"Damnation," she muttered.

"Going somewhere, Jo Beth?"

She whirled around. Colter was standing just

inside the cabin, a polish rag in his hand and a grin on his face. She was caught. There was nothing to do but make the best of it.

"Colter. What do you mean, sneaking up on me?"

"I didn't sneak, I walked."

"What in the world are you doing here?"

"I might ask you the same thing."

"I'm a guest. Family connections, you know."

"Ahh, yes. Now I remember. Your brother is an old friend of the Donovans."

"Right."

"Since you're his guest, I'm surprised you didn't chat with Jim Roman last night."

"Was that Jim? We'd only met over the phone." It was hard to make her eyes look wide and innocent when each one was holding about two pounds of cold cream. But she tried.

"Yes. He's my best friend—or was until today."

"Oh?"

Colter was beginning to enjoy this encounter immensely. Jo Beth had always been refreshing, but she'd never been more delightful than when she was trying to play innocent. And it was certainly an act. Two meetings in two days were more than chance. He suspected that Fate was getting a hefty push from Jim Roman.

Colter leaned against the wall and relaxed. He hadn't felt so relaxed since he'd left the White Mountains.

"You're cute with a shiny face, Jo."

She put both hands on her cheeks and they came away slick. "Wrinkle cream. I was going to try to pass it off as the glow of youth, but I figured you'd know better."

She lifted the sheet higher around her neck to cover her gown. In the process, she uncovered her feet.

Colter looked down at her socks and smiled. "Are you cold?"

At that very minute she was burning up, but she didn't tell him so. "Would you believe pink fuzzy feet?" He chuckled and she grinned. "October through April I wear socks to bed. If my feet are warm, I feel warm all over."

"I can think of better ways to keep warm in bed, Jo."

"I can too, Colter."

They studied each other, wary now. His fingers tightened on his polish rag and hers tightened on the sheet. His need was so urgent that he had to work hard to keep from walking across the small cabin and lowering her to the bunk. A small shred of nobility saved him.

"I should get back to work. I promised Jim I'd polish his brass."

"Then I'll try to keep out of your way. . . . I don't want to bother you."

"You don't want to bother me?" He crossed the cabin in three quick strides. With one hand he smoothed her tumbled hair away from her face. "You don't want to bother me, Jo?" he asked again, softly. "Knowing you're on the same planet bothers me. Having you in San Francisco disturbs me." With his fingers woven into her hair, his hand caressed her scalp. "Being in the same cabin with you is almost more than I can bear."

She closed her eyes. This wasn't the way the game was supposed to work, but, ahhh, it felt so good. She'd enjoy his touch a while longer, and then she'd resume her role.

His hand left her hair and roamed down the side of her face. Then he traced the delicate bone structure along her jaw.

"You are wonderfully and beautifully made, Jo Beth McGill."

Suddenly he released her. She sank onto the bunk, still holding the sheet high around her neck. With her eyes closed, she felt rather than saw him leave. Slowly she unclenched her hands. The sheet slid onto her lap.

She took a deep breath. It was time to get out of her stupor. She'd never get Colter Gray Wolf by being easy.

"I had a patient once who wore a Winnie-the-Pooh gown."

Jo Beth's eyes snapped open. Colter was leaning against the door, his face unreadable as he watched her.

"I thought you had gone."

Still watching her, he continued as if she hadn't spoken. "She was only twelve."

Jo Beth put her hand over the design on the front of her cotton flannel gown and unconsciously rubbed Pooh Bear's head. "I've had this gown for years. Andrew gave it to me when I was in the hospital with pneumonia. He said Pooh Bear would make me feel secure and loved."

"Does he?"

"No. He does nothing except cover me and keep me warm." She met his gaze.

Colter didn't speak for a long while. She could hardly breathe. She held herself so still, she got a cramp in her toes. Finally Colter broke the silence.

"I envy him," he said, and then he was gone.

Jo Beth lay back on the bunk, drained. She felt as if she'd given blood to the Red Cross and they'd accidentally taken all she had.

"Heaven help me," she said. "What in the world am I going to do?"

She lay there a while longer, working up her courage. Finally she decided that she hadn't come all the way to San Francisco to fall into Colter's arms and be sent away again. *This time*, she was going to be in charge.

She hurried with her bath, then quickly jerked on her clothes—old jeans and a Mississippi State sweatshirt. Dressing to thrill had given way to dressing in a hurry.

She piled her hair on top of her head, secured it with a maroon ribbon, and hurried into the galley. Toast and eggs tempted her, but she didn't have time for all that. She hadn't heard a sound from Colter. For all she knew he had packed his polish rag and gone back to his own houseboat. She poured herself a large glass of juice, then gathered her ammunition and headed to the top deck.

She was out of breath by the time she reached topside. To her relief, Colter was still there, his back to her, silently working on the brass. It was time for her big show.

She put a fancy smile on her face and sauntered past him. She made enough racket so he'd be certain to hear. Sure enough, just as she was undulating past, he looked up. She put an extra hitch into her walk and glanced out of the corner of her eye to see how he was taking it all. The polish rag was still, but so was his face. Too late, she wondered whether he preferred twenties vamps or fifties innocents. It was funny that she didn't know that about Colter.

"Good morning, again." She put all the cheer she could muster into the greeting.

He didn't speak. He leaned against the railing and watched as she pulled out a deck chair and placed her booty on the small table. Without looking at him, she selected the most succulent strawberry in the bowl and lifted it to her mouth. She curled her lips around it and took a big bite. She savored the berry, and then slowly, ever so slowly, she took the uneaten half away. Bits of pulp clung to her lips.

She made her eyes wide and innocent as she looked up at him.

"Did you come to tempt me, Jo?"

"Yes." She bit into the berry again, never taking her gaze off him. He watched her elaborate flirtation with the berry. When she had eaten the whole thing, she flicked her pink tongue around her mouth. "Want some?"

"How can I refuse such an invitation?"

He slowly set aside his polish rag. Colter was not without a sense of drama himself. He seemed to take forever to cross the polished deck. When he reached her, he leaned one slender hip against the table edge.

"Are you sure you don't want to retract that offer?"

"I'm positive." She reached for another berry.

He watched her dig into the bowl. When her hand was in midair, he reached out and caught her by the wrist. Leaning over the table, he closed his mouth over the strawberry. He didn't bite into the juicy flesh immediately, but kept his mouth clamped so that the tips of her fingers were against his tongue.

He held her that way, watching her. A bead of sweat popped out on her forehead and a hot flush stained her cheeks. He moved his tongue back and forth, dragging it with agonizing slowness across her fingertips.

He held her fingers in his mouth so long, the strawberry began to disintegrate. Finally he was forced to release her fingers and swallow the berry juice. But he kept his hold on her wrist.

"Do you want another one?" she asked.

He didn't reply immediately but held on to her, looking deep into her eyes. Memories of September nights in Arizona hung between them.

His hand tightened. Leaning across the table, his face close to hers, he said, "Don't offer what you're not ready to give, Jo."

Her heart raced, but she refused to back down. "Don't take what you're not ready to keep, Colter."

The truth of what she had said struck him in the gut. He had taken her, had claimed her for his own, and then he had let her go. She had every right to be angry. Was that why she had come here, he wondered. For revenge? Though it was totally out of character for her, he had to consider it as a possibility. After all, when he had asked her to wait for him, she'd told him she didn't know what she would do.

"Why are you here, Jo?"

"I told you. Business."

"I think that's only part of the truth."

She smiled at him. "You have your secrets and I have mine."

"Jo . . ." He stopped speaking. He could tell her no more now than he could on White Mountain. Releasing her wrist, he stepped away from the table. "Eat your strawberries. They're good for you."

"Doctor's orders?"

"Friendly advice."

"Is that all we are now, Colter—friends?"

It was a long time before he spoke, and when he did, his voice reminded her of the music of the mountains. "That's all we are, Jo . . . for now."

Never taking her gaze from his, she reached into the bowl. The strawberry she selected was overripe and very juicy. She took her time eating it. She sucked on the berry, bit into it, savored it, and finally swallowed the last bite. Then she very carefully licked her lips, like a satisfied cat.

It was more temptation than Colter could bear. He came around the table and lifted her from the chair. His hands gripped her shoulders and his face was tight.

"There's a better way to clean your mouth, Jo."

He bent down and very carefully traced her lips with his tongue. All the breath left her body. He lifted his face just a fraction from hers, and she could still feel his warm breath when he spoke.

"Strawberries taste better on you. . . . I think I'll have some more."

And he did. This time he didn't lick her lips; he took them in a kiss that was so fierce and hot, it burned all the way to her toes. When he finally let her go, she was actually panting.

He stepped back, and she put one hand over her puffy lips.

"Is that what you wanted, Jo?"

"Colter . . ."

"Last night you asked what you would get if you flirted with me. Does that answer the question to your satisfaction?"

"No." She dragged the last bit of McGill bravado from somewhere inside her shaky self. "If that's the best you can do, then I've wasted money on these strawberries."

Amusement lit his eyes and turned up the corners of his mouth. He didn't merely pull her into his arms—he took her captive. He held her in such a way that she could feel every inch of his body, from the muscular calves and thighs all the way up to the well-toned chest. While his mouth claimed hers, his hands roved over her back. There was magic in his fingers. They massaged and explored and aroused until she was dizzy with desire. She felt as if the houseboat were rocking in a stormy sea.

Once more she became Earth Mother and he became Father Sky. He filled her senses, even as he had once filled her body. The only thing missing was the music of his native poetry. He kissed her silently this time. There on the deck of the houseboat, Jo Beth discovered that she had followed Gray Wolf to San Francisco and had found Dr. Colter Gray instead.

She ran her hands through his newly cropped dark hair. She had loved the braids, but the hair didn't matter. The thing she missed about her Colter was the Apache music he'd carried in his soul.

Still in his embrace, Jo Beth made her vow: She'd have it all. She'd have her worldly Dr. Gray and her poetic Gray Wolf, or her name was not Jo Beth McGill.

When Colter finally let her go, she stepped back and smiled at him.

"That's much better. I especially enjoyed what you did with your hands."

"Then we'll have to do it again sometime, Jo."

He turned and walked away. His departure was as quiet as his arrival had been. The exit was dignified and dramatic, worthy of all his famous ancestors. Jo Beth might have been disheartened, except for one thing: He'd forgotten his polishing supplies.

She smiled and plucked another strawberry from the bowl. Her assault had just begun.

Colter didn't even stop to change his clothes. He left Jo Beth and went directly to the hospital, driving his Porsche through the streets with the same flair that he rode his stallion through the mountains.

When he stepped off the elevator onto the third floor, Nurse Martin pursed her fat lips and shook her finger at him.

"You know good and well that overworked doctors are supposed to stay at home on their days off."

"Martin, you know better than to tell a doctor what to do." He chucked her under the chin. "You're not getting enough sleep. Is that arthritis still bothering you?"

"No more than that burr under your saddle is bothering you."

He laughed. Nurse Martin always had the last word with him.

"Give me the charts on Briggs and Gladney and keep that lonely-hearts advice to yourself."

"Humph. Not that you'd take advice if I gave it to you." She handed him the chart and looked pointedly at his feet. "Moccasins?" With one finger she reached out and touched a spot on his shirt collar. "Stains? Have I missed something, Doctor Neat? Is the world coming to an end?"

"Strawberries, Nurse Martin. Have you ever heard of them?"

"Yeah. But I've never heard of you getting a stain on your immaculate person." She rolled her eyes. "What is this world coming to?"

He gave her an enigmatic smile and disappeared down the hall with his charts.

Nurse Martin turned to Nurse Turner. "What did I tell you, Tilly? Our Dr. Gray is in love."

"In love? Not Dr. Gray. He donated his heart years ago. There's nothing in that beautiful bronze chest of his except a time clock."

"How do you know what his chest looks like? You been up to something and holding out on me?"

"Don't I wish." Tilly Turner beseeched the cool white hospital ceiling with her eyes. "It stands to reason, Geraldine. Anybody with gorgeous skin like that is bound to be bronze all over."

Nurse Kemp came on duty just in time to hear that last remark. She adjusted her cap and picked up her ever-ready blood kit.

"You two would do well to forget about Dr. Gray's assets—whatever they may be—and get back to work." She adjusted her cap once more and marched down the hall, stiff-backed.

Geraldine Martin rolled her eyes. "Nurse Vampire's back."

Colter's patients were impressed by his unexpected visits. They seized their opportunities to regale him with their latest aches and pains and to spin endless tales of woe about the hospital food.

He listened to them patiently. Then he spent an hour reassuring them. Finally he carried his charts to the nurses' station. Fortunately, Nurse Martin was down the hall answering a distress call. Otherwise he would have been treated to another of her quizzes.

He left the hospital and drove to his clinic. It was closed on Sundays. He let himself in the back door, and without switching on lights, made his way to his office. He sat in his swivel chair and propped his feet on his desk.

He'd been fooling himself to believe that he could put Jo Beth out of his mind by working today. He crossed his ankles and leaned back to think. He loved her; that hadn't changed. He wanted her—more than ever, if that was possible. And she wanted him.

He smiled. There was no doubt about her desire. What he didn't know was her intention. Since he couldn't read her mind he'd have to deal with facts. She'd turned up at the baseball game and the marina. Coincidence? He didn't think so. She was stalking him.

The sudden revelation brought his feet crashing to the floor. Why hadn't he seen that before? She was using his technique—the Indian way of courtship—but with her own unique flair. The second stage was giving presents. And the third stage . . . He stared off into the distance thinking about the third stage of Apache courtship. He couldn't expect Fate to keep dropping Jo Beth on his doorstep. If he covered her with his blanket this time, he'd for damn sure better not let her go. Instinctively, he knew that he wouldn't get a third chance. This was it.

He opened his desk drawer and took out a notepad and his favorite pen, the thick one with the big tip. He divided the paper into two columns. Then he began to list problems and possible solutions.

The process took hours. When he had finished, his future was outlined in bold black letters.

He put the pad in his desk drawer and the pen in the pencil holder. Then he leaned back in his chair, satisfied.

"Jo Beth McGill, I'm ready to let you conquer me." He chuckled. "But I promise you, it won't be easy."

Ten

Jo Beth knew Colter's habits. Jim and Hannah Roman had been knowledgeable and more than willing to help.

She sat on the deck of Jim's houseboat, waiting for Colter to appear. Jim had said Colter spent hours each night sitting on the deck of his boat, communing with nature.

Jo Beth glanced at her watch. It was already eleven-thirty. If Colter didn't show up soon, there wouldn't be any nature left to commune with. Clouds had been building in the sky since afternoon. Now they all but obscured the few stars that had been brave enough to shine.

Her feet tapped impatiently on the polished wood, and she was just getting ready to go below when she saw a shadow across the way. She leaned over the railing and squinted into the darkness.

"Out for a stroll, Jo?"

Colter's voice floated across the bay, rich as music and bright with good humor.

"I'm enjoying the cool night air. How about you?"

"I'd enjoy it more if you were by my side."

"Is that an invitation, Colter?"

He laughed. "Do you need one, Jo?"

She didn't reply immediately, but lolled against the railing and lazily lifted her hair off her neck. She knew exactly what the sight of her hair in the moonlight did to Colter Gray Wolf. Only a sliver of moon was visible tonight, but it was enough. She stood directly in its path and fanned her hair through her fingers.

"If that's for me, I approve."

She leaned over the railing once more and pretended innocence. "If what's for you?"

"That performance." He clapped his hands, and the sound was magnified across the water. "Bravo, Jo."

"Thank you. I do love an appreciative audience."

"Do you love music, too, Jo?"

"Yes."

He walked to a small table and turned on a portable radio. The melodic strains of "As Time Goes By" wafted across the bay. Colter reappeared at the railing.

"We missed our dance in the mountains, Jo. May I have this one?"

"Won't that be hard to do with you over there and me over here?"

"I can remedy that."

Once more he left the railing of his boat. She saw him walking across his deck and watched while he disappeared over the side. She was still leaning forward, looking across at his boat, when he tapped her on the shoulder.

She whirled around. "How did you get here so quickly?"

"Apache secrets." He caught her shoulders and gazed down at her. "You're wearing the blue dress."

"I felt festive tonight."

"Any particular reason?"

"It's this city, I guess. It's very romantic. Especially here on the water."

His right hand slid down to caress her bare back. She shivered.

"It's a little cool for a bare back, Jo, even in California."

She'd been thinking the same thing as she'd shivered in the breeze for the last two hours, waiting for him. But, of course, she didn't tell him so.

"I have warm Mississippi blood." She wet her lower lip with the tip of her tongue. "Hot blood."

"Let's find out just how hot your blood is." He put one hand on her cheek, and she lifted her face toward his. He leaned down until he was only an inch from her mouth, and then he chuckled.

She jerked her head back.

"Did you think I was going to kiss you, Jo?"

"Absolutely not."

"You were all puckered up."

"I never pucker, Colter."

He smoothed back her hair, watching the play of moonlight in its bright strands. "I remember, Jo." His voice had gone as low and gentle as the murmur of a mountain stream. "You never pucker. You open." He traced one finger around her mouth. She wet his finger with the tip of her tongue.

He brushed his lips against her temples. "Do you want to keep playing the game, or shall we put an end to it?"

"What game?"

He leaned back and looked into her eyes. He had his answer. She wanted to play out the game. He could understand that. He'd done more than send her away in the White Mountains. Without meaning to, he'd rejected her. He understood that now. He also understood that she had to get him back in her own way. She had to have her moment of triumph.

He'd give it to her.

"Let's dance, Jo."

He put his arms around her waist and held her close. Her dance rhythms were the same as her love rhythms, beautifully fluid and impeccably timed. He leaned his cheek on her hair.

"I've never danced with you, Colter."

"Do you like it?"

"Immensely."

His arms tightened. For the first time since he'd left White Mountain, he felt Apache music stir his soul. He leaned close and began to murmur in his native tongue.

Jo Beth almost lost her step. The words she had waited so long to hear were falling upon her ear like a gentle spring rain. She had no idea what the words meant, but she understood them anyhow. They were the poetry of Colter's Indian soul. They were words of mystery and beauty. They were words of love.

Her spirit soared. She had found Gray Wolf. He had not vanished in this city of neon and noise—he had merely been waiting for her to bring him out.

When the words stopped, she tilted back so she could look into Colter's face. "That's beautiful. Will you tell me what it means?"

"In the red light of evening I come to you. With wings of eagles I lift you up and carry you into the sky."

The music of his radio stopped, but still they danced. Her skirts rustled in the breeze off the bay and her hair whispered around her face. In that moment, if he had held out his hand and said 'Come,' she would have gone with him. If he had called her Yellow Bird or told her she was his woman, she would have gone into his houseboat and never looked back.

But he didn't. Instead, he dipped her low, so low that her hair hung down and touched the deck. With one strong arm supporting her back, he leaned close to her face.

"Could you live in San Francisco, Jo?"

"Is that a rhetorical question?"

"A point of interest."

"It's so far from home . . . so far from Mississippi." He raised her up and held her at arm's length. "But if the right man asked me," she continued, "if someone I loved very much said to me, 'Jo Beth, come make your home with me,' I would."

"What if that someone asked you to live in the desert or in the mountains?"

"Any specific desert? Any specific mountains?"

"Arizona."

She tried to keep the hope from shining in her eyes and trembling in her voice. "Then I would say yes. Home is not a place, Colter. It's where love abides."

"You once told me you didn't believe in love."

She almost said, *That was before I met you, Colter.* But she remembered her purpose just in time. Make him ache for her, make him wait for her. And then, when she was certain he would never want to send her away again, only then would she speak of love.

"How can I know?' she said lightly. "It takes two to make love."

"So it does, Jo." He ran his hands lightly over her bare back. "If I had a tepee, I would take you captive." He leaned over and ran his lips down the side of her throat.

She started to speak, and he moved his mouth

to the front of her throat. His tongue found her pulse spot. She felt her resolve weakening.

"But I don't have a tepee," he whispered against her throat. Then he straightened, smiling. "Good night, Jo."

He left as quickly as he had come. She stood on the deck of her borrowed houseboat, astonished. *She* was the one who was supposed to say no. What was happening to the game? "Playing hard to Get" had worked out fine, but Phase Two, "Willing but not Easy," wasn't working out so well.

She kicked a deck chair. "Damnation."

"Did you say something, Jo?"

Colter's voice floated to her through the cloudy mists. She looked up, but could see nothing except fog. She assumed he was standing at his own railing.

"No," she said. "I just bumped into something on my way to bed. Good night, Colter."

"Good night, Jo."

Jim Roman was just finishing his first cup of Monday morning coffee when his phone rang.

"Jim, I'm going to have to change my plans."

"Jo Beth, is that you?"

"Yes. I hope I didn't wake you."

"No. My little warriors have been up for an hour. What's up?"

"Coming to your houseboat was a really grand idea. And it's working . . . up to a point. But what I really need is a place where I can have Colter's undivided attention. I thought about it all last night, and here's what I want to do." She told him her plan.

After he had finished laughing, he agreed to help her. He had just hung up and was reaching for the coffeepot when the phone rang again.

"Jim, it's Colter."

Jim chuckled. "Love does make early birds, doesn't it?"

"Has Jo Beth already called you?"

"She has. How long did it take you to figure out what was going on?"

"Not long. Everything clicked when I saw her on your houseboat. Jim, I don't intend to lose her again. Tell me her plans."

"Hey, I'm double-crossing you, remember?"

"I'm asking for a double double cross. A man who would haul an antique bathtub up a mountain to win the woman he loves is capable of anything. Now, tell me her strategy so I can plan mine accordingly."

"Whatever happened to Fate, Colter?"

"Fate is sometimes fickle. I'm not leaving my love life in the hands of Fate this time around."

"Neither is she, buddy." Jim outlined Jo Beth's plans.

Colter was not surprised when the call from ER came late that afternoon. In fact, he'd been expecting it for two hours and had begun to wonder whether Jim was pulling yet *another* double cross. His friend did have a wicked sense of humor.

"Dr. Gray, this is Nurse Langley in ER," the nurse in charge of the hospital emergency room identified herself. "There is a patient here who insists on seeing you. She's adamant."

"Who is she?"

There was a pause while Nurse Langley consulted her chart. "A Jo Beth McGill. She was brought in by friends, a Jim Roman and his wife, but quite frankly I can't see a thing wrong with her. All her vital signs are fine and she looks healthy as a horse."

"What's her complaint?"

"They're all very vague. First it's her heart and then it's her back and then it's her head." Nurse Langley sighed. "I told her that Dr. Wright is the physician on duty, but she refuses to see him. What shall I do?"

"We can't be too careful these days. Too many lawsuits. I have one more patient to see, then I'll be right down."

Colter stifled his chuckle. Nurse Langley had done beautifully. Everything was in place—the staff was informed, a room in the unused wing of the hospital had been readied, and he was set to capture his Yellow Bird for all time.

Jo Beth hadn't bargained on this wretched hospital gown when she'd hatched her plan. She readjusted the tacky gown, trying to arrange it so only her best body parts showed through the openings. Then she looked at her watch for the fifteenth time. She'd been waiting an hour.

"Colter's not coming," she said.

Hannah Roman, who was beautiful even in her ninth month of pregnancy, patted Jo Beth's hand. "Don't worry, he'll be here."

Jim took his eyes off Hannah long enough to add his opinion. "Why don't you use some more of that powder? You don't look sick enough to me."

Jo Beth repowdered her face and practiced going into a decline on the narrow examining table. "How is that?"

"Perfect," Hannah said. "You'll have Colter eating out of your hand."

The door swung open, and Dr. Colter Gray strode in. "Did someone mention my name?"

Jo Beth got so excited, she almost forgot to

decline, while Hannah and Jim started talking at once.

Colter held up his hand. "Please. If you two will leave me alone with the patient, I'll find out what's bothering her."

Hannah and Jim slipped from the room, closing the door behind them. Colter put his fingers on Jo Beth's pulse and gave her a serious, doctorly look.

"Jo Beth, I didn't expect to see you here, especially since you looked so healthy last night." Still holding her wrist, he bent close and peered into her eyes. He noticed that her pulse accelerated. Stifling a smile, he said, "What's the matter? Too much dancing?"

"Too much night air, I guess." She went into the coughing routine she'd practiced all morning. Then she put a limp hand on her brow and tried for a swoon.

Colter slipped his arms under her shoulders and pulled her into a close embrace.

"Do you do this for all your patients, doctor?" Her voice was muffled against his white coat.

"I believe in total care."

"Then you must be very much in demand."

"See how well it works. Your voice already sounds stronger." He laid her back down on the examining table.

Jo Beth was going into another decline when she noticed her powder on the front of Colter's lab coat. She hastily changed the decline to a coughing fit, complete with flailing arms. It was no accident that her arms flailed mostly at the telltale powder. When it looked like she had destroyed most of the evidence, she sank back onto the table and put a hand on her brow.

"Do you think it's serious, Colter?"

"I think it's very serious, Jo. The treatment could take a long time. Maybe even years."

Jo Beth narrowed her eyes. That foxy Colter was on to her again. He knew darned good and well there was nothing wrong with her except an overactive libido and a huge talent for drama. Still, that didn't change things. She and Colter Gray Wolf had a few scores to settle, and they might as well settle them in the hospital arena with plenty of witnesses.

She made a failed attempt at sitting up, then put her hand dramatically over her heart. Next she put on her dying-calf-in-a-hailstorm look and made her voice as weak as last Tuesday's tea.

"What are you going to do about my condition?"

Colter put one large, warm hand on her chest. "Is your heart bothering you, Jo?"

She started to say no, for even she knew that she couldn't have pneumonia and heart trouble to boot without being near death's door. But just when she was going to deny that malady, Colter started massaging her chest. The swoon she went into this time was not practiced.

She lay on the hard, narrow table, fighting a losing battle to look sick. "What your hands can do through a hospital gown ought to be considered illegal, Colter."

"It's part of your cure, Jo." He kept up the massage. "I can already see a noticeable improvement in your color."

Heat had put two bright spots in her cheeks, shining through all the layers of powder.

"Would you prescribe these massages on a weekly basis?"

"Twice daily should do it."

"I feel better already. Shall I set up another appointment with you?"

"I leave this sort of thing to the nurses and the interns." He patted her knee. "Don't worry about a thing, Jo, they'll take good care of you."

He turned to leave and was almost at the door before she could find her voice.

"Colter!"

With his hand on the doorknob, he turned to look at her. "Did you forget to tell me something, Jo?"

"No. You forgot to tell me. Where are you going? What are you planning to do about me?"

"I'm admitting you, Jo. We need to run tests to find out what's wrong with you before I prescribe treatment . . . except the massages, of course." He smiled at her. "As to where I'm going . . . There's a wonderful seafood restaurant on the bay. I was going to invite you to go along. Too bad you'll be stuck here in the hospital. See you, Jo." He left, whistling.

Jo didn't know whether to laugh or to cuss. She'd gotten what she wanted—to be in the hospital, where she would have Colter's undivided attention—but it hadn't turned out exactly the way she had planned.

Hannah Roman poked her head around the door. "How did it go?"

"I wish I knew." Jo Beth swung her feet off the table and reached for her shoes. "Where's Jim?"

"He and Colter went for a cup of coffee. They invited me, but I wanted to talk to you."

"I could sure as heck use some talking to." Jo Beth began to dress. "I'm not an old hand at this, and I keep getting the feeling that Colter is always one step ahead of me."

"He is." Hannah put her hand over her stomach. "The baby's kicking." She waddled to a chair and sat down. "Jo, Colter knows that you're here to pursue him and capture him, so to speak."

"It's more than that. I want to prove to him that people in love stick together, no matter what sort of problems they're having." Jo bent over to tie her jogging shoes. "How does he know?"

"Jim, of course." Hannah smiled indulgently. "You have to understand. Their friendship goes a long way back. They're as close as brothers."

"Colter would have guessed anyhow. He's too smart not to."

"What I think we should do is double-cross the double-crossers."

"That's the best idea I've heard yet. I'm open to suggestions, Hannah."

"Then, here's what I think we should do. . . ."

Colter made sure Jo Beth was settled in her room, where he knew Nurses Martin and Turner would take good care of her.

He made his hospital rounds, then left the hospital, laughing at the audacity of the woman he'd pursued in the desert. He intended to go back to his houseboat, change clothes, then have a long, leisurely meal at a good seafood restaurant. But by the time he'd gotten back to his boat, he knew he wasn't going to do that.

He changed into jeans, a denim shirt, and moccasins, prepared a quick meal in his galley, then headed back to the hospital.

Nurse Martin pursed her fat lips when he showed up. "Back again, Dr. Gray?"

"Yes. I have to see my patient."

Nurse Martin didn't dare lift an eyebrow when he picked up Jo Beth's chart and left the station. But as soon as he was out of earshot, she walked over to Nurse Turner, who was sorting pills for the nine-o'clock rounds.

"Tilly, I'd love to know what's going on between those two. He wouldn't tell me much, except that it was sort of a joke."

Tilly grinned. "Maybe I'll saunter down that way to see if she needs anything."

"Try the bedpan, that always shows the true state of their health."

Nurse Tilly Turner left the station and eased down toward Room 306. The first thing she heard was the laughter. That was enough to stop her dead in her tracks. Dr. Colter Gray was one of the most serious physicians she knew. He smiled at his patients, of course, and he was always friendly with them. But she had never heard him laughing the way he was right now.

She eased open the door. She didn't see it as "sneaking." Not exactly. She just wanted to get a candid view of what was going on. What was going on gave her another jolt. Dr. Gray was actually *sitting on the bed holding the patient's hand.*

He suddenly looked up and saw her.

"Nurse Turner, is there anything you want?"

He didn't even get off the side of the bed. That was one for the records. Tilly adjusted her cap and put on her most professional air.

"I came by to see if the patient wants anything—juice, ice, bedpan?"

Dr. Gray laughed again. Then he did the most astonishing thing: He leaned over, in an intimate way, and said, "How about it, Jo? Do you want Nurse Turner to fetch the bedpan?"

The patient had one of the prettiest smiles Tilly had ever seen. "I can still manage that on my own, and I expect to get better every day, now that you're taking care of me, doctor."

"She doesn't need the bedpan, Nurse Turner." Dr. Gray was still smiling. "Anything else?"

"No, I'll just tidy up." Tilly walked over to the

bed and straightened the covers, on general principle. Then she puttered around the lavatory and fiddled with the bed rails. "Everything seems to be shipshape. Good night, Jo . . . Dr. Gray."

She couldn't get back to the nurses' station fast enough. Geraldine looked up from her charts.

"Well, if that face is any indication, I'm in for quite a story."

Tilly sat down and put her hand over her heart. It was going ninety miles an hour. "You'll just never believe what I saw. In all my years of knowing Dr. Gray, I never thought I'd see it."

"If you don't tell me in about two seconds, Tilly Turner, you're never going to live to see another day, let alone another year."

"Well, first of all . . . you should have *seen* that nightgown she was wearing: It was a beautiful blue and so sheer I could look right through it and see everything she's got. And that's just what Dr. Gray was doing. Looking down at that gown like he was going to rip it off with his bare hands. Oh, he was laughing and joking, but Lord! were those eyes of his sizzling."

Geraldine pushed her charts aside and propped her fat chin on her dimpled elbows. "I'm panting. Tell me more."

"Well, he was sitting on her bed, and she had one hand on his knee. It was meant to look casual, even accidental, but when I was straightening up the soap dish I watched them in the mirror. She was *running her hands down Dr. Gray's legs.*"

"I've been waiting fifteen years for somebody to ring Dr. Gray's chimes, and when it happens, I'm not even there to see it." She sighed. "Next time *I'll* offer the bedpan."

"You're not going to believe what happened next."

"Tell it before I have heart failure."

"He said something, real low like, and I know he didn't mean for anybody to hear except Jo. But I heard it."

"What did he say?"

"Lord, how do I know? He was talking Indian or something."

"Shoot, I'll bet that was the best part. What else, Tilly?"

"I ran out of excuses to hang around. That's all I know."

"If he's not out of there in another fifteen minutes, I'm going down to see exactly what's going on." Geraldine gave a dramatic sigh as she picked up her charts. "I hope it's something good. I'm so tired of listening to everybody's aches and pains I don't know what to do."

Colter couldn't bring himself to leave Jo's bed. He was beginning to get used to that shockingly sexy gown, so that he didn't have to stare so much, but he couldn't bear to deprive himself of her hand upon his knee.

The odd thing about her hand being on his knee, he mused, was that she didn't even seem to be aware of what she was doing. She was the same laughing, friendly Jo, but she was different in a way that he couldn't explain. True, she was beautiful and sensuous and, of course, she still had her hand on his knee, but none of that seemed to be directed specifically at him. Even his bit of Apache poetry hadn't moved her to more than a casual smile.

He began to wonder if Jim had been wrong. If they'd all been misreading Jo Beth McGill.

"I'm so glad you put me here, Colter. And I'm looking forward to another of those nice massages."

"I could give you one now."

"Please." She held up her hand. "Don't bother." She smiled sweetly. "I'll wait for one of the nurses . . . or some nice young intern."

That statement was enough to send Colter off the bed. He prowled the room. It was one of the few times in his life he hadn't known exactly what to do. Finally, after she had watched him in complete silence for a small eternity, he sat in the uncomfortable chair beside her bed. The chairs had been designed to discourage long hospital visits, but he wasn't about to let a chair defeat him.

"Are you staying a while longer, Colter?"

"Yes. Since you're from out of town and don't have anyone else . . ."

He left the sentence hanging in midair, for Jo Beth chose that moment to yawn and stretch her arms above her head. The stretch almost brought him out of his chair. He clenched his fists at his side. As if the stretch hadn't been enough to make him forget he was in a hospital, she executed a series of upper-body movements that almost sent him right through the ceiling.

"Sleepy, Jo?"

"I could use a little sleep." She lifted one languorous arm and let it sort of float through the air. Colter fought another battle with control. "Women in my condition need their rest, you know."

"No doubt." He tried to read her mind in those wide, innocent blue eyes. He half-rose from his chair, then sank back down.

"You're leaving, then?"

"You're sure you don't need anything, Jo?"

"Positive." She smiled, but it was not the smile of a sick woman.

"Then . . ." He got out of his chair and started toward the door. "Good night." He put his hand on the door handle and turned it slowly, waiting for her to call him back. She didn't, and he left quickly.

He walked the familiar halls he'd walked a thousand times before, but it was the first time he'd never seen a thing. Habit told him when to turn left at the nurses station.

"Oh, Dr. Gray." Nurse Martin lifted her hand and hailed him. He never even heard her.

His moccasins didn't make a sound as he walked quickly toward the elevator. It came on the first punch of the button, and whisked him down to the parking garage. Habit carried him to his slot where the Porsche waited, and habit carried him through the streets to the bay. Only when he reached his houseboat did he come to his senses.

He sat down on his bed and stared at the dark porthole on the opposite wall, thinking. Maybe Jo Beth would start trying to capture him tomorrow.

Eleven

Jo Beth had just had her morning bath and changed into a sizzling black-lace gown, when Colter walked through the door. She didn't even have time to jump back into bed and recline.

"What brings you here so early, Colter?"

"Your massage."

Jo Beth thought he sounded and looked a little tense. That was good, because she couldn't stand much more waiting. If he didn't make his move soon, she'd have to.

"I thought that intern . . ."

"No. He's busy with other things."

"You came to tell me I won't be getting a massage. How *sweet* of you, Colter."

"I came to do your massage, Jo . . . Are you going to get into bed or shall I carry you?"

She hopped into bed. She hadn't counted on this turn of events. Maybe it was a good sign.

He bent over her, and she saw all his fire and passion in his face. It was an unspoken invitation that she found hard to resist. She closed her eyes to shut out the sight, but then he put his hands on her. His touch was not professional—it was pure seduction. A sigh escaped her lips.

"Relax, Jo. Just relax." She felt him slip her straps over her shoulders. His hands moved across her bare skin like music.

"Ahhh, Colter." One more minute, two at the most, and she knew she'd be pulling him down onto the bed, all her resolutions forgotten.

"Dr. Gray, Dr. Gray. Report to obstetrics." The harsh voice over the intercom brought the massage to a halt.

Jo sat up, her straps still hanging over her shoulders. "Obstetrics, Colter?"

"It must be Jim and Hannah."

"The baby." Jo hopped out of bed and grabbed her robe. "I'm going with you."

Jim Roman met them in the hall outside the waiting room. His shirt was buttoned up wrong, his hair was mussed, and his shoes didn't match. He grabbed Colter's hand and squeezed.

"What if something happens in there? What if she doesn't make it? What if something is wrong with the baby?"

"Hannah is a perfectly healthy woman doing what hundreds of women do every day. It's going to be all right." Colter led him to a chair in the waiting room. "How long has she been in there?"

"Since three o'clock this morning."

"I'll scrub and go in." Colter had just started to leave when Hannah's doctor came to the door. "Jim Roman, you have a nine-pound baby boy. Mother and son are both doing fine."

"When can I see them?"

"You can go in to see your wife now. The baby is on his way to the nursery."

In his joy, Jim forgot his recent need for friendly bolstering. He left to see Hannah.

"I love babies, Colter," Jo Beth said. "Let's go see."

Colter led Jo Beth to the nursery. He pointed to the crib that said "Roman" and glanced briefly at the baby. It looked like all newborns, its color was good, and it had a lusty howl. The person who held his interest was Jo Beth.

She had her face pressed against the glass, cooing at the baby. She positively glowed. What would she be like if the baby were hers? he wondered. He'd heard of the radiance of motherhood, but he'd never paid it any attention. He glanced at the tiny bundle that so fascinated Jo Beth. Suppose that were his son in the nursery? Would he have his shirt buttoned wrong and his hair uncombed?

Suddenly Colter was filled with a longing he'd never experienced. He longed for a home with curtains at the windows and gingerbread in the oven. He longed for the welcoming kiss of a wife and the happy laughter of children. *His* wife. *His* children.

He'd never dreamed of those things before. He'd only dreamed of making Jo Beth his woman. He glanced at her radiant face once more. It was time to put an end to all the waiting, to put an end to all the games.

"Jo Beth." When she looked up, he held out his hand to her. "Come."

She followed him. Whether it was out of habit or because of the look on his face, she didn't know. Nor did she care. It was time, time to clear the air.

He hurried her through the halls and back to Room 306. Then he closed the door and leaned against it. He tugged Jo Beth's hand and pulled her closer. When she was standing before him, he put his hands on her shoulders.

"You're my woman, Jo. You always have been."

Her eyes widened, but she didn't say anything.

"What we had in the desert was not a September affair," he continued. "It was love. I love you, Jo, and I want you to be my wife. I've always intended for you to be my wife."

Still, she was silent. He smiled.

"I assume silence means consent."

Color shot into Jo Beth's cheeks. "Well, you assumed wrong." She jerked herself out of his grasp and put her hands on her hips. She had a hard time to keep her lips from trembling. She had just turned down the thing she wanted most in the world—a proposal from Colter. She wanted more, so much more.

She closed her eyes and gathered her strength. It was time for the big gamble. Her eyes snapped open. If she could have seen any signs in his face, she would have felt better. But Colter was inscrutable, as always.

"Love means trust, Colter, and sharing. You shut me out when you had a problem. You sent me away. When I marry, it will be to share the bad times as well as the good." She bit her lip and added, "I don't even know what you've decided about your future."

"I'm going to tell you, Jo."

"When?"

"When I have all the details worked out."

"I can't live like that, Colter, never knowing what's going on in your mind, never knowing where your next 'journey of the soul' will take you."

"I'm rebuilding the clinic."

"I found that out . . . but not from you."

His hands tightened. "Jo, you said you'd be willing to live anywhere with a man if you loved him enough."

"Colter . . ." She reached out and tenderly stroked his face. "Don't ever think that I don't love you. I do. You made me believe in love. You made me believe in miracles." Her fingertips circled his lips. "When I went back to Mississippi I lay awake at night, listening for the call of the turtledove, knowing it would never come. I didn't cry. I just lay there listening."

"I'm sorry, Jo."

"I'm sorry too." She pressed her palms against his cheeks, and her expression was fierce. "I love you more than I ever thought it possible to love a man, but I can't be your pretty little plaything, somebody who is good enough to share your blanket but not good enough to share your life. I want to share your life."

"I want you to share my life. That's why I'm asking you to marry me."

"Then talk to me, Colter."

He pulled her into his embrace, pressing her so close she could hardly breathe. "Don't you think I would tell you if I had everything worked out?"

She stayed in his arms a while longer, feeling the steady beat of his heart underneath her cheek. She'd gambled and lost. It was time to go.

"Let me go, Colter." He released her and she stepped back. "I think this charade has gone on too long. I'm going home."

"Back to the houseboat?"

"No. Home to Mississippi."

He retreated into one of his long, deep silences. Then he turned and left the room.

Nurse Turner saw him coming. "Good Lord,

Geraldine. Look quick, because you'll never see it again. Dr. Gray is actually *showing* his anger."

Geraldine Martin looked up. "That's not anger, Tilly, that's a cyclone and an earthquake all rolled into one." She stuck her head into her charts and pretended to be working when he stopped at the desk.

"Nurse Martin."

"Sir!"

"See that the patient in Room 306 does not leave this hospital. I'm holding you personally responsible."

He left without another word.

Colter had always given his patients more time than they actually required. Today, however, he merely saw to their complaints and prescribed their treatments. By midafternoon, he had cleared his office. Leaving his astonished secretaries and nurses in charge, he left the clinic.

Movement was what he needed. Action. Since he didn't have his white stallion, he rode his Porsche through the streets. He drove hard and fast, thinking, thinking. On the reservation, life had been simple. It had been defined by rules and taboos and enhanced with myths and poetry. In the world of the white man, life was complex, with no rules, few taboos, and a set of laws that smart people knew how to circumvent and manipulate. The myths and poetry were there, but they were sometimes hard to find admidst the roar of parties and the clamor of television.

Jo Beth was a product of the white world. She was complex, and he'd tried to impose simple rules of behavior on her. Now he'd lost her.

No! his mind shouted. He wouldn't lose her. He

refused to let her go. But how could he get her back? He drove for a while, letting his mind drift, trying to open himself to the truth, trying to find the answers. When the answer came to him, he knew it had been there all along, waiting to be discovered.

His hands relaxed on the wheel and his foot lightened on the accelerator. The winds of change swept over his soul, and they felt good.

Jo Beth paced the floor for an hour, waiting for Colter to come back. Then she realized he had patients to see. She'd give him a while longer. She picked up her book and tried to read. The clock ticked on, mercilessly slow. Finally she decided he was not coming. She had truly lost Colter Gray Wolf.

She knuckled her hands into her eyes. She couldn't cry, not yet, not until she was safely on a plane. She jerked her bag down from the hospital closet and slung it onto the bed.

Nurse Martin came into her room with her chart. "Going somewhere, Jo Beth?"

"Home."

"I'm afraid that's not possible. Dr. Gray hasn't released you."

"I don't need a release." Jo Beth wadded her gowns and tossed them into the bag. Then she threw her toiletries in after them, not caring whether the powder spilled and the toothpaste squirted out.

"Why don't you finish packing, and I'll give his office a call."

"Thank you, Nurse Martin. You do that."

Geraldine Martin hurried down the hall, wringing her hands. "Lord, Tilly, Dr. Gray is going to skin me if that woman leaves." She sat down at her desk and picked up the phone. The receptionist in his office told her to try his home. She got his answering machine at his home. She was about to try his office again when she spotted him strolling down the hall.

"Dr. Gray, I've been looking everywhere for you."

He leaned across the desk and smiled. "Nurse Martin, I want to talk to you in private."

Jo Beth had her hands on her suitcase, and was ready to walk out the door, when she realized she was still wearing her black-lace gown and robe. She jerked off the robe, then began to lower her gown straps.

"I'll do that for you."

Her hands stilled and her heart stopped . . . almost. Colter Gray Wolf was standing just inside her doorway. He was wearing jeans, moccasins, and a buckskin shirt. All he needed to look as if he had stepped down from the canvas of a Remington was his white stallion.

He walked silently across the room, taking his time. When he was within touching distance of her, he stopped.

"Hold out your hand, Jo Beth."

She wanted to believe in the triumph of true love, but as always, his face was unreadable.

"What's the matter, doctor? Do you want to take my pulse?"

"No." He placed a small object in her palm and closed her fingers around it. "I want to give you this."

It was a small glass bird, its wings tinted yellow.

"Colter . . . it's beautiful." She caressed the shiny

surface of the bird, daring to hope but not daring to guess his mind.

"So are you, my Yellow Bird."

He came to her then. Taking her free hand, he gently pulled her into his arms. "From the time I stalked you in the desert, I knew you would be my woman. It took me a long time to realize that claiming you entailed responsibilities for me." He stroked her hair. "I'm ready to share my life with you. I'll hold nothing back."

"Are you planning to leave San Francisco for the mountains, Colter?"

"I don't know that yet. At first I was certain I would, because of my promise to my father. And then I realized it was not a promise I would have made if he had been well."

"It wasn't a promise—it was a kindness. You're a kind man, Colter Gray Wolf, and I'm happy to accept your proposal."

"If you hadn't said yes, Jo, I would have taken you captive." He kissed her then, and would have gone on kissing her forever, but he knew there were things still unsaid. He lifted his head and looked down at her. "I'm considering several options, Jo. Setting up scholarships and letting interns work the clinic; working there part-time myself; finding a good physician looking for a more relaxed practice, almost a semiretirement. I simply don't know yet what I will do." He looked down at her and smiled. "What *we* will do."

"We'll work it out together." She leaned her cheek on his chest and caressed his back. "A year ago my father would have loved you as I do. Now, he'll never understand."

"I can live with that, if you can live with my mother trying to turn you into an Apache." His hands moved to the straps of her gown.

"Colter, what are you doing?"

"What does it look like?" He slid her gown off and reached for his shirt.

"You wouldn't dare."

"I dare . . ."

She smiled. "What will the nurses say?"

"If any of them can get past Nurse Martin, they'll say plenty."

He pushed the button that lowered the hospital bed. Jo Beth started to laugh, but Colter put a hand over her mouth and pulled her down onto the bed. "Shhh."

The sheets settled over them. He caught her face between his hands and whispered, "I will cover you with my blanket and make you mine."

He did. The musical whisper of Apache poetry filled the room, and there was no one to hear except the small yellow bird on the nightstand.

Epilogue

The entire McGill family had gathered in the White Mountains for the opening of Colter's clinic. Jo Beth and Colter stood in the center of the newly painted reception area, talking to the doctor who would be setting up his practice there.

"I can't tell you what this means to me, Dr. Gray . . . not having to wear a tie every day." Dr. Richard Raymond, only recently of Detroit, pushed his hand through his gray hair and chuckled, showing a line of white, even teeth. "It's a beautiful place to spend the sunset years of my life, and working with you six weeks every summer will be the icing on the cake. You've quite a reputation."

"Thank you, Dr. Raymond." Colter shook his hand, then led Jo Beth away.

"That's what I think, too, Dr. Gray. You've quite a reputation."

When he thought no one was looking, he swatted her bottom. "Behave yourself, Mrs. Gray."

"Don't you know that women of twenty-nine always misbehave?"

He laughed. "Then it would be best if I took you to a more private place."

He took her hand and started toward the door. On the way they passed Silas McGill. He had his camera trained on Little Deer, who was leaning against a desk, posing for all she was worth.

"Dad-blamed it, Pocahontas." Silas fussed with the camera lens. "Can't you hold still? I need this picture for evidence."

"I don't care what you need it for, Silas McGill." Little Deer plumped up her hair and smoothed down her dress. She was rather pleased to be mistaken for such a famous woman. "I need it to show my grandchildren how good I looked on this auspicious day."

Colter and Jo Beth smiled and slipped out the door. Chieftain was waiting for them. Colter vaulted onto the white stallion and held out his hand.

"Come."

Jo Beth smiled up at him. "You haven't lost your touch, I see."

"Apaches never do."

Jo looked at his extended hand. "I'm not sure a woman in my condition should be vaulting onto horses."

"Your condition?" Colter lost all his inscrutability. When he slid off the horse and caught her in his arms, he was like every other husband hearing good news. He looked as if he had personally discovered America. "Yellow Bird, are you trying to tell me that we're going to have a baby?"

"Well . . . I'm not sure . . ." When she saw his face start to fall, she added, "Perhaps if we worked on it some more . . ."

He lifted her gently onto the stallion and mounted behind her.

"I know the perfect place, Yellow Bird."

She leaned against him and sighed. "I've always wanted to ride off into the sunset with a good-looking man."

THE EDITOR'S CORNER

It's been a while since we acknowledged and thanked the many people here at Bantam who work so hard to make our LOVESWEPTs the best they can be. Aside from our small editorial staff, members of the art department, managing editorial department, production, sales, and marketing departments, to name a few, all contribute their expertise to the project. The department whose input is most apparent to you, the reader, is that of our art department, so I'd like to mention them briefly this month.

Getting the cover art exactly right isn't an easy task. No two people ever envision the characers the same way—and think of how many people read our books! Our art director, Beverly Leung, knows how important it is for you to have a beautiful cover to look at. Her job starts by commissioning an artist for a particular book. The artist is given a description sheet prepared by the author herself. After models who most closely resemble the characters are selected, a photographic shoot is done, and from those photos the artist/illustrator creates first a sketch and finally a painting for the cover.

During the entire process Beverly works to ensure we—and ultimately you—are pleased with the finished artwork. She's done a fabulous job since taking on the assignment, and it's reflected in the gorgeous covers we're able to bring you. Thanks, Beverly.

Now on to the good stuff! Next month's LOVESWEPTs feature heroes so yummy, anyone on a diet should beware!

Kay Hooper weaves another magical web around you with **THROUGH THE LOOKING GLASS**, LOVESWEPT #408, the next in her *Once Upon a Time . . .* series. Financial wizard Gideon Hughes fully intends to shut down the carnival he had inherited. But when he arrives to check it out, he's instantly enchanted by manager Maggie Durant—and balance sheets loose all interest for him. Gideon is intrigued and unnerved by Maggie's forthrightness, but something compels him to explore the deep and strange feelings she stirs in him. Then Maggie openly declares her love for Gideon and in so doing, lays claim to his heart. Amid clowns, gypsies, and magicians, Gideon and the silver-haired siren find the most wondrous love—and together they create their own Wonderland.

In **PRIVATE EYES**, LOVESWEPT #409, Charlotte Hughes delivers the kind of story you ask for most often—one that combines lighthearted humor with powerful emotion. Private investigator Jack Sloan resents being asked to train his
(continued)

partner's niece, Ashley Rogers. He takes one look at her and decides she doesn't belong on an undercover assignment, she belongs in a man's arms—preferably in his. But he soon discovers he's underestimated the lovely single mother of two. Ashley works harder than he ever imagined, and her desire to win his approval tugs at his heart—a heart he thought had long ago gone numb. Charlotte puts these two engaging characters in some hilarious situations—and also in some intimate ones. Don't miss this very entertaining romance!

Sandra Chastain often focuses on people living in small towns, and her knack for capturing the essence of a community and the importance of belonging really makes her books special. In **RUN WILD WITH ME,** LOVESWEPT #410, Sandra brings together a wicked-looking cowboy, and a feisty lady law officer. Andrea Fleming has spent her life in Arcadia, Georgia, and she's convinced it's where she belongs. Her one attempt to break away had ended in heartache and disaster. Sam Farley is a stranger in a town that doesn't take kindly to outsiders. He doesn't understand how someone can have ties to a place—until he falls for Andrea. She makes the handsome wanderer crave what he's never known. This is a touching, emotional love story of two lost people who find their true soul mates.

Deborah Smith's heroes are never lacking in good looks or virility—and the hero of **HONEY AND SMOKE,** LOVESWEPT #411, is no exception. Ex-marine Max Templeton could have walked off the cover of *Soldier of Fortune* magazine. But when he encounters Betty Quint in a dark mountain cave, he finds in her one worthy adversary. Betty is a city girl who has moved back to the town of her ancestors to return to the basics and run a small catering business and restaurant. She can't believe the man beneath the camouflage and khaki is also the local justice of the peace! Of course, there's no peace for her once Max invades her life. But Betty is looking for commitment. She has dreams of marriage and family, and Max runs his wedding chapel as if it's all in fun—and with the knowledge that marriage is definitely not for him. You'll love being along for the ride as Betty convinces Max to believe in a perfect future, and Max proves to Betty that Rambo has a heart!

Doris Parmett has a lot of fun inventing her wonderful heroes and heroines and researching her stories. For her latest book she visited a local cable television station and had a great time. She was asked to appear on a talk show,

(continued)

and it went so well, they invited her back. Absorbing as much atmosphere and information as she could, Doris returned to work and created the love story we'll bring you next month. In **OFF LIMITS**, LOVESWEPT #412, Joe Michaels and Liz Davis make television screens melt with their weekly hit show. But off camera, Liz fights to keep things all business. Joe refuses to deny the sexual tension that sizzles between them and vows to prove to the vulnerable woman behind the glamorous image that a man can be trusted, that their life together would be no soap opera. These two characters produce a whirlwind of passionate emotion that sweeps the reader along!

What woman hasn't fantasized about being pursued by a ruggedly gorgeous man? Well, in **BLUE DALTON**, LOVESWEPT #413 by Glenna McReynolds, our heroine, Blue, finds the experience exhausting when tracker Walker Evans stalks her into the Rockies. Blue is after the treasure she believes her father left to her alone, and Walker thinks his is the valid claim. When Walker captures her, she can't help but succumb to wild sensation and has no choice but to share the search. Confused by the strength of her desire for Walker, she tries to outsmart him—but her plan backfires along with her vow not to love him. Only Glenna can blend exciting elements of adventure so successfully with the poignant and heartfelt elements that make a story a true romance. Don't miss this unique book!

We're pleased and proud to feature a devoted LOVESWEPT reader from down under as our Fan of the Month for June. Isn't it wonderful to know stories of love and romance are treasured and enjoyed throughout the world!

Hope your summer is filled with great reading pleasures.
Sincerely,

Susann Brailey

Susann Brailey
Editor
LOVESWEPT
Bantam Books
666 Fifth Avenue
New York, NY 10103

FAN OF THE MONTH

Wilma Stubbs

It gives me great pleasure to represent the Australian fans of the LOVESWEPT series, and there are many as evidenced by the fact that one has to be early to get titles by favorite authors such as Kay Hooper, Barbara Boswell, etc.

I have been reading LOVESWEPTs since early 1984 when the Australian publisher distributed a booklet comprised of excerpts from the first titles. I was hooked—and impatient! So I wrote a plaintive letter to New York for a publication date, and the nice people there sent back a letter full of information.

As the mother of two semi-adults with their associated interests and friends, and the wife of a man who has worked shift work for twenty-five years, I've always found romantic fiction to be my favorite retreat. LOVESWEPTs cover a broad range of moods—from the sensuousness of Sandra Brown to the humor of Billie Green to the depth of Mary Kay McComas to the imaginativeness of Iris Johansen, particularly her Clanad series with the delightful touch of mystique.

I have often recommended to troubled friends that they read some of the above authors in order to gain a balance to their lives. It seems to refresh one's spirits to dip into other lives and gain a better perspective on one's own.

60 Minutes to a Better, More Beautiful You!

N ow it's easier than ever to awaken your sensuality, stay slim forever—even make yourself irresistible. With Bantam's bestselling subliminal audio tapes, you're only 60 minutes away from a better, more beautiful you!

__	45004-2	**Slim Forever**	$8.95
__	45112-X	**Awaken Your Sensuality**	$7.95
__	45035-2	**Stop Smoking Forever**	$8.95
__	45130-8	**Develop Your Intuition**	$7.95
__	45022-0	**Positively Change Your Life**	$8.95
__	45154-5	**Get What You Want**	$7.95
__	45041-7	**Stress Free Forever**	$8.95
__	45106-5	**Get a Good Night's Sleep**	$7.95
__	45094-8	**Improve Your Concentration**	$7.95
__	45172-3	**Develop A Perfect Memory**	$8.95